N

Prim

Improper

Deirdre Sullivan is many things: a riddle within a mystery within an enigma, a champion napper and the guardian of two ungrateful guinea pigs who keep vowing to destroy her. She would like to see them try, the little fools. They have NO IDEA who they're dealing with. She enjoys acting, reading, writing, crafting and daydreaming about the Viking who will one day rescue her from her life of drudgery. Also, cake. She really, really does enjoy cake.

Illustration by Jana Allen

PRIM
IMPROPER

by

Deirdre Sullivan

Little Island

First published 2010
by Little Island
an imprint of New Island
2 Brookside
Dundrum Road
Dublin 14

www.littleisland.ie

ISBN 978-1-84840-948-4

British Library Cataloguing Data. A CIP catalogue record for this book is
available from the British Library.

Book design by Fidelma Slattery

Printed by CPI Group (UK) Ltd

Little Island received financial assistance from
The Arts Council (An Chomhairle Ealaíon), Dublin, Ireland.

10 9 8 7 6 5 4 3

To Diarmuid O'Brien, my friend of friends. Nom.

Acknowledgements

★ First and foremost I want to thank Siobhán Parkinson without whom this book would literally have not been written. Her support, encouragement and general awesomeness on every level have meant so much to me. I could show my appreciation by standing beneath her window in a trenchcoat with a ghettoblaster but I think we'd both rather I didn't.

Deirdre O'Neill - Editor and magician for behind the scenes ★ organisation and having a nifty business card.

★ Elaina O'Neill — for knowing (amongst other things) the difference between a colon and a semicolon and using her powers for good instead of evil.

★ All the other people at Little Island who did stuff, I do not know your names, but there was stuff to be done and you,

————————————, did it magnificently. (the space above is for you to write your name in so you can show this to people. 'Look!' you will no doubt exclaim proudly 'I totally got acknowledged by some writer of moderately-priced fiction for teens and possibly also tweens! Imagine the high fives that await you! If you do not work at Little Island and you have written your name in this space in a vain attempt to be funny I will hunt you down and punish you. No joke. Your days are numbered, matey.

Jana Allen — for being lovely and artistic, despite (or perhaps because of?) coming from a country where people are ★ often barefoot. Also her daughter Bella for being an adorable pirate.

★ Diarmuid O'Brien — for making me cups of tea and listening to me read what I just wrote. Also for being better than almost everyone else in the world.

⭐ Maria Griffin - for being the best fake sister a girl could ask for.

Camille de Angelis, Ciara Banks, Suzanne Keaveney and ⭐
Samantha Keaveney - for reading it before anyone and
offering advice. Really good advice too, not the stupid generic kind
you buy in shops. You are all fantastic and I am lucky to know you.

⭐ Adrian Frazier, Tom Hall and all the people at the MA in Drama
who told me to keep on writing. Guess what? I did!!

Writer's Soc. in NUIG, where I first read stuff and ⭐
didn't get laughed at, except when it was supposed to be
funny. Also where I met Ciara Banks (see above) and Diarmuid
O'Brien (see above).

⭐ Mary, Julianne, Danielle, Jacinta, Eileen, Deirdre (not me, the
other one) who were there when this all began, over scones and tea.

My Nana - Alacoque Sullivan for being an amazing example of ⭐
strength and creativity. I am proud to be your granddaughter.

⭐ My father Tim - for being kind, brave, clever and never
forgetting to ask me how the writing was going, even when it
wasn't. Thanks for the genes.

And finally to my mother Mary - for believing in me when ⭐
I wasn't sure I believed in myself and never giving up on
me, even when I wanted you to. Your tenacity and enormous heart
amaze and humble me.

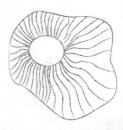

MY FATHER AND HIS HOUSE

Sometimes I wonder if my father loves his moustache more than he loves me. He's had it longer. He grew the thing before he met my mother. I know because I've seen it in the pictures that she used to show me when I was smaller and not as shy about asking awkward questions.

My father doesn't brush me with a special comb twice a day, or anoint me with a specialist pomade that he orders off the internet. (Not that I'd want him to. Because *eww*.)

My dad's house – the house where I live now too – is big and old and fancy. The people that he bought it from must have spent a lot of time restoring it – this is what my father says anyway – so that modern people who like to pee indoors could live in it. They must have really loved it, those people; all the walls were beautifully coloured, with stencilled silhouettes and little painted flowers, wild and hothouse; really, really beautiful to see.

'Girly,' declared Captain Moustache, and immediately he hired a team of men to sit around drinking tea I'd made and eating breakfast rolls in between spurts of painting everything in various shades of white, with names like 'Lily of the Valley', 'Ermine', 'Baby Teeth' and 'Miscellaneous Clouds'.

I made the men leave the walls of *my* room alone. I threatened them with biscuit withdrawal and then cried down the phone to my dad, who was in the middle of an important meeting (I checked his appointment diary before I made the call), as leather sofas and glass-topped coffee tables replaced cosy rocking chairs and furniture with claws instead of stumps.

My room is gorgeous – in an old-fashioned kind of way. It makes me feel like a 'domestic'. (You know, a little olden-days servant girl straight out of a novel by Frances Hodgson Burnett. Someone who gets up at five in the morning to light the fires for 'them upstairs'. Although I suppose 'them downstairs' would be more accurate, because my room is upstairs at the very tip-top of our house, in the attic.) It is stuffed with bits of furniture left behind by the people who used to live here. I like this. It feels like I have company. Company apart from Roderick, that is.

Glossary: List that explains words that are new or hard or spelled funny. Often boring and not worth reading as it is fun to make up your own slightly cheeky (oh my!) meanings for new words; for example *assonance*, which does not mean 'behaving like a bottom or a donkey or the glorious marriage of both: a donkey's bottom' but I would be happier if it did and so that is what it means to me, and anyone who dares to disagree is being totally assonant. Like an ass. I am too lazy to write a proper glossary but I do like explaining words so that is what

I will do now and then. It will be a sort of glossary, or 'lip-glossary', if you will, where words are explained and my father is insulted where applicable. Like now!

POMADE: An oily mix between gel and cream that some people like to put on their hair. I've heard (and stop me if this disgusts you) that some poor idiots even put it on their stupid little moustaches. Isn't that hilarious? The world surely is a crazy place!

RODERICK

Roderick's house is in my room. It balances easily on my big sturdy bookshelf, halfway between floor and ceiling. It's more of a cage than a house really, but I always call it his house because I don't like to think of Roderick living in a cage. Even if it is a purple and white two-storey rat paradise, with a small fleecy hammock and a chewable wooden tunnel where he can go for privacy, to scheme his ratty schemes and plan his ratty plans and ... um ... poo. I also keep a box of tissues cage-adjacent, because he loves to pilfer them greedily. (It stops him nibbling other more valuable things like my CD cases.)

He is a terrible scamp. Mum called him 'the inimitable Roderick', or sometimes 'Señor Roderigo' when he was being particularly dashing.

We got Roderick from this guy my mum was seeing last year, when he was only a small and baldy fellow. Roderick, I mean. (My mother's boyfriend back then, Dave, was man-sized and had lots and lots of hair.) Roderick was only tiny the first time I saw him, wriggling like a maggot into his mother's warm tummy. There were lots of little rat babies, but he was definitely the boldest one, and I picked him out as mine on that very first day.

Me and Mum went to the pet shop together and got all kinds of fancy rat-paraphernalia for when we were allowed to take him home. He was an absolute terror right away, all courage, staging complicated breakouts and nibbling his way right into one of the sofa cushions. Mum wasn't sure we could handle such a criminal mastermind in our lives, but I thought he was only fantastic, and he soon melted Mum's heart by balancing on things that were very high up, wearing what Mum called his 'You'll never catch me, copper!' face. He always came down eventually, especially after we learned to ignore him and eat delicious food pointedly until his inevitable surrender. 'They always come crawling back,' Mum would drawl, in a fancy-pants British accent. I'd roll my eyes at her and happily scratch my little rat-man's ears.

My father is not gone at all on my furry room-mate. He doesn't like Roderick, and for that reason he will almost never venture into my room. Which is one more thing I love about having a pet rat. Initially I worried that my father's negativity would have a dreadful effect on poor Roderick's self-esteem. But he seems happy enough to chomp

DASHING: An attractive feature in a man; a way to describe someone who would sweep you off your feet in the good way, not by tripping you and then pointing and laughing with all his stupid friends. Handsome pirates are dashing, but none of the boys in my class are.

PARAPHERNALIA: Stuff that relates to other stuff. Like Dad has lots of *Star Wars* paraphernalia, and I mock him because of it. Dad hid all of it before Hedda came over for dinner. Mum always kept her cycling paraphernalia in the hall for me to trip over on my way out the door.

down all the rat food and fancy two-ply tissues that the moustachioed one's money can buy, and that's the main thing, I suppose. Anyway, the old man doesn't seem to care much about me either, and I'm absolutely grand.

Moving house can be difficult for an animal, but I suppose his little house is still the same, just in a different location. I'm keeping an eye on him, though, in case he gets rat-depression, which I read about online one day when he wasn't touching his food. I think we'll be okay.

WHAT TO DO NEXT

I don't know if I'm ready to go all the way to 'big girl school' yet. I don't have all my books and Mum isn't around to get them for me. Plus my hairy-faced father is always working, except when he is out for dinner with his stupid, boring friends or his girlfriend, Hedda. I call her Hedda Lettuce and sometimes Hedda Cabbage. But not to her face because I haven't met her yet.

I left the booklist that came in the post from my school on Dad's desk, but he hasn't mentioned it yet at all. He probably wouldn't even know what it is. I'll need a new uniform too, in a bigger size. I'm getting wider, spreading out and changing (I'm what they call a late developer, which is kind of irritating because I am developing fine, thank you very much. I quite like being able to jump up and down without getting walloped in the face by things that are both soft and womanly. Sadly, those days are almost behind me). I don't feel any bigger, though. If anything I should be getting smaller. Less important. More intangible and strange, like how I feel.

My Catholic schoolgirl costume (ooh-er) is not overly bad as uniforms go, although the black tartan skirt and/or trousers are a bit creepy and unflattering. There's also a plain white shirt and a dark greyish V-neck jumper with the crest on it which says something in Latin, which is the school motto and probably means 'Sit down and shut up'. It'll be a nice change from the navy gymslip etc. that I've worn since time began. Well, since time to go to school began, so for, like, eight years. Since I was but an innocent flower of five, full of hope and joy and wonder and a longing to impress my teacher with my mad fingerpainting skills. Needless to say, those days are a long, long way behind me.

I think I need a feisty new look to go with my new uniform and brand spanking new levels of academic pressure. The Old Man of the 'Tache has already made noises about this being the first year of the Junior Certificate cycle, which is the practice run for the Leaving Cert, and how I'm not to be slacking off at all but am to keep my nose to the grindstone, which sounds painful and kind of creepy. *He* should keep *his* nose to the grindstone; it's longer and infinitely less attractive than mine, like a cliff jutting out of the middle of his face.

I'm thinking about dyeing my hair – well, getting it dyed *for* me, so I don't end up with colouredy ears and forehead. I need a haircut anyway. I'll tell Dad and he'll probably throw the money at me and not even notice when I emerge all glossy-haired and chic. He has to drop me to the doctor tomorrow, so I might get it done then. I hate going to the doctor (she is a head doctor, not a doctor for when you are feeling under the weather). I wish I could bring Roderick with me but he'd only wee in my bag or run away. Probably both.

THE QUESTIONABLE PRACTICES OF MY DOCTOR

My doctor's office is boring and stupid, just like she is. It's all brown and grey and dreadful. There are books and things on the shelves, but I bet they're all props just to make her seem more human and approachable. I bet she hired actors to be in the family photos on her desk. I bet she doesn't have children at all and if she does, they hate her.

She has a bowl of jelly beans on her desk, but I can never take one even when she offers because once I saw a fly land in the bowl and she just let it sit there and didn't swat it away or anything and that is so disgusting. Whenever I come back to find a different arrangement of jelly beans now, I think of someone chewing on a fly-eggy jelly bean, gulping it down and having no idea how repulsive and diseased it was and hoping she would offer them another. *Yuck* is all I can say. *Yuck yuck yuck yuck yuck.*

8

HAIR: THE ARGUMENT!

My new hair is lovely. I don't look like myself at all. I look like Snow White. Or a different girl with really shiny hair – a vampire or a Bratz doll or something. Of course, Mr Whiskers (my father, not a delightful and imaginary cat) wasn't impressed. He was all assertive and called me 'young lady', which I didn't think parents called children in real life. (It's certainly not something Mum could have said with a straight face.)

'It's just a haircut, Fintan,' I said airily. (I had been practising.) 'Chill.'

Again, that is not something I would normally say in real life. It was a knee-jerk reaction to the 'young lady' thing, fulfilling his expectations of how young people speak. At least I didn't add 'the beans'.

'*Someone* in this family has to have good hair,' I concluded, 'or we'd be shamed in the eyes of the parish and wouldn't be able to go to mass any more.' He makes me go to mass, now that I live 'under his roof'. Mum would so not approve. Actually I have no idea why I was so surprised by the 'young lady' thing; it totally fits his profile.

As soon as I turn sixteen (only three more years!!) I'm going to get a tattoo of skeletons doing unspeakable things on top of motorcycles. While wielding flaming swords. That's the level of rebellion I'm looking for. Having nice hair is just a matter of *taste*. (I think my new ebony tresses have made me more confident and assertive.)

He had the gall to look offended and ran his fingers through his own semi-solid 'do. (He had to wipe them off after; he uses *waaay* too much oily goo that comes in pots – see 'pomade'.) Anyway, apparently I have to 'cop on to myself' and I 'have a lot of growing up to do'. And he'll 'let me know' what my punishment is going to be. (Maybe he will peck me to death with his enormous grindstone-sharpened nose?) Honestly, as if living with him wasn't punishment enough, never mind everything else that came before.

And, to quote the man himself, 'another thing': I'm thirteen years old. Of COURSE I have a lot of growing up to do, especially seeing as I don't even wear a bra yet (yeah, I know, sad little late developer me). Although I do, as of this afternoon, have an extremely fine-looking head of hair.

I can't believe they let people like him even *have* children. It's not fair. None of this is even a little bit fair and I'm so, so sick of it. As soon as he leaves, I am going to feed Roderick one of the hairy scary père-y's expensivest novelty ties. My father is a man who wears novelty ties. Agh. *AGGGGGGGGGHHHHHHHHHH!*

At least I'll have something to tell Doctor call-me-Triona at the next session.

10

GALL: Bitter, sour, horrid feelings. The stuff inside you that makes you go 'gah!' when you see someone with nicer stuff than you or 'muhahahaha' when they trip over and break their stupid face. Gall is not nice and if someone does something bad to you, like laugh when you trip over and break your stupid face, you can talk about 'the gall of them!' to your friends while plotting a terrible revenge which will cause Laughy McTrip-face to exclaim 'the gall!' and plot their revenge which is how wars get started.

It's a vicious circle.

MY PAL JOEL

Joel is fun, even though he will not be joining me at the school for grown-up ladies and gentlemen, preferring instead to go to one that doesn't let females in because we would distract the young chaps from their studies with our endless flower-arranging and talk of boy-bands and glitter. Besides, in the REAL world men never, ever, ever have to deal with girls being around unless they want to. Just ask Fintan.

Joel's mum and I both wanted him to go to the same school as me, but he had done a lot of research into St John of God's, especially the rugby and rowing teams, which is funny because he neither rows nor rugbies, and I doubt he's going to take it up without a personality transplant of some sort. In the long-gone, childish, halcyon days of Ye Olde Primarye Schoole, we were both scared of PE, and we *both* pretended to have lady trouble to get out of it, even though we were only in third class and he was not a lady but a small boy – and even if he *had* been old enough, there is no such thing as man-struation. Silly bear. That's kind of why I love him, though.

I texted him after the row with Dad yesterday and he said I should come stay the night at his house, watching scary films and eating junk. His parents always let me stay the night and because

11

they feel sorry for me, we can probably get a take-away. It's nice to be in a normal house, which is small and messy and warm. Our house here, Dad's house, is always a little cold. Well, it is in my room anyway. In the attic. I've started putting a fleece over Roderick's cage at night in case he catches pneumonia, or the dreaded rat-flu.

Joel has been my best friend since playschool, where we used to fight because we both wanted to marry this boy in our class, Kevin. (He was pretty foxy for a three-year-old, as I recall, all Batman schoolbags and runners that light up.) Joel doesn't like being reminded of that, maybe because he decided a long time ago that runners that light up were 'more tacky than fun'. (Think whatever you like, Joel, I will always consider them the knees of the bees).

Anyway, we've both moved on, and now we like horror films we're far too young to watch and playing dress-up, which we're probably a little bit old for. Joel has got an amazing dress-up box. We used to really like putting false moustaches on his baby brother Marcus and then taking pictures and laughing at him (not in a mean way, in a 'Look, it's a teeny-tiny circus strong-baby with a handlebar moustache' kind of way), but then I moved in with the man who sucks the joy out of life, and the moustache thing lost some of its comedy value. (Some, not all, because, hey: baby with moustache!)

But I wasn't allowed to go to Joel's because I am being punished. Hairy-faced Father was not into the idea of releasing me from his tender care, because I am not allowed to have any fun until he says so, or forgets all about it. (So for about a day or two, then.) It's still annoying, though.

THINGS I DO NOT LIKE: A NON-COMPREHENSIVE LIST OF YUCKS

Having to talk about my feelings to the queen of bland. Dr call-me-Triona. She charges, like, €100 an hour or something as well. I would prefer Mr Moneybags to just give me the money so I could buy an iPod and an army of rats to do my bidding and listen to my woes.

Being felt sorry for (except when I can use it to get stuff like food and permission to do things). Just before the holidays, when I went back to school, it was horrible. I felt like I had two heads or was about to be shot out of a cannon. If all eyes are going to be on me, I want them to be on me because of my talent and beauty (ha!) instead of just being horrible gossipy spotlights. 'How sad does she look? Is she going to cry? Isn't it awful soon for her to be back?' They don't have to say anything, students or teachers, but I know what they're thinking when they *look* at me. And I really, really, really cannot stand it. But now it will be a new school, where no one – except the many losers who are following me from primary – will know my story. Unfortunately, some of them (Karen and her coven) are dreadful gossips. Pah!

That I'm going back to school in a week's time. Granted, it is a new and shiny school, which could possibly be filled with hotly brooding young men for me to share my pain and ultimately my body with (ooh-errr), but I still don't want to go. Sorry boys, I am not ready for that level of physical and emotional commitment, or, you know, to get out of bed before noon.

14

Human statues. They're all over the place in summertime and there's something really smug about them, especially when someone gives them money and they move. It makes me shudder.

Having to live here. I miss my old house where everything wasn't horrible and fancy. It was the raggediest, cosiest place in the world.

Being 'not allowed' to do things. By the Great Wizard of Giving Permission himself, Daddy Dearest. What a joke! He has no idea how to raise a child and he acts like he's all up on this parent stuff. And he's not. He's such a faker. I mean, where was he when I actually needed someone, before, back then? I don't even know – probably golfing or getting an Indian head massage.

Indian head massages. There is something kind of yucky about a man who pays another man fifty euro to rub his scalp. Hairbrushes do that for free. And also: Neither the masseur guy nor my father have even the teeniest drop of Indian blood. If I ever get an Indian head massage, I expect turbans, saris and exotic sitar music. And maybe tiger balm. Mum was a great believer in tiger balm.

People who are all 'You have a *rat*? That is SO disgusting.' (Like evil Karen in my class and now in my year – will she never let me rest?!) Although it is a good way of weeding out the people who I would never in a million years want to be friends with anyway, not even if they begged. My Roderick's existence must be bigot-free and full of joy. As should every pet's.

Being shipped off to boarding school one of these years. Mark my words, it will happen. And I won't have Joel or Roderick or anyone to talk to. And Fintan can just go back to being a part-time dad, which is all he signed up for in the first place.

My face. I'm 'the image of' my dad, only mercifully free of his Roman nose. He calls it Roman. I call it ENORMOUS. I'd like to be 'the image of' my mum. Or just myself. I'd settle for myself.

WHAT MUM WAS LIKE

Lovely. But not all the time. She could get really catty when she was tired, or hungry, or disappointed.

She had long goldeny-red hair and four holes in each of her ears. The corners of her mouth turned down a bit when she smiled. She had freckles on her nose and on her shoulders. She wore jewellery, but not make-up, or not often anyway. She liked old films and cooking and sitting on the grass in gardens or parks in summertime. She didn't like washing up or going to bed early.

Her name was Bláthnaid, and everyone called her Bláth, which is the Irish for flower. She loved flowers, so it fit her perfectly. I called her Mum, though. I have the same surname as her. My dad is a Hamilton, but Mum and I were Learys. I still am one, as I refuse to join 'team Hamilton'. Mind you, Mum's still a Leary as well. That's what the head-stone says anyway.

She had a really stupid laugh, like she was going to cough something up. A hairball, maybe. Listening to her laugh would usually make me laugh, even when the joke wasn't funny at all. She cycled to work and when I was little I had a special seat at the back of her bike, and I was always a bit scared when I was on it, but a good kind of scared. A safe scared, when you know you're being minded.

She was always broke, but she still made sure that I had everything I needed, even if a lot of it was second-hand. She used to cut our hair herself. I wish I had kept some of her hair to have now. It was so shiny and so soft, even when it was all tangly and mussed up.

She had a boyfriend every now and then, but I was always the most important thing: her best friend. If I didn't like whoever she was seeing she would never bring him home, only out to movies and restaurants and things.

She was really clever. She could read Old English (the kind that people spoke in the *really* olden days back when men wore tights and women did not judge them for this, but rather found it foxy and delightful – we have come a long way since then). She could do really hard sums too and she kept household budgets in a little book. She didn't like taking Dad's money, and she would put it all in a savings account for when I got older or needed something expensive.

She had really pale eyebrows and eyes that were brown and green at the same time.

She liked peppermint tea and in our house we had an aloe vera plant – I don't know where it is now. I want to remember everything about her: she liked the smell of custard powder and dandelions and petrol. She was scared of earwigs, because she thought that they would crawl into your ear and make you deaf. She spoke French but she couldn't roll her R's. She kept her fingernails very short and clean. She could play three songs on the guitar and she would have taught me, but I was always too impatient.

Her favourite dress was blue with poppies on it. She called it her 'garden party dress'. Dad hired some women to go through her clothes and give them to charity shops. All I kept were that dress and a cardigan I sleep in. I used to love rambling around charity shops with Mum, but now I'm scared I'll just see all these bits of her on hangers there and no her anywhere.

I would have liked to hang on to more of her books. She used to write little notes in them and underline bits. Dad kept the first editions for me, for when I get older, and I filled a cardboard box with a few more. I thought I would have more time to choose; I didn't realise that it was all happening that day.

Mum was always ten minutes late collecting me from places. She used to decorate her cheesecake with melted chocolate and jelly babies. Her favourite food was Pad Thai. She couldn't get it right when she made it herself, but she never stopped trying to make her version as nice as the one from the takeaway that we sometimes ordered on special occasions. She wore an orangey-lilac perfume that her friend Sorrel, who blends scent, had made for her birthday. She loved me to bits but she didn't always like me. And she was real. And she *is* real. I want her to stay real.

19

SINGLE SEX ...

In two days' time I will be stuck in the land of homework and discontent. I am a sad rabbit. Sniffle. Sniffle. Sniffle. On the plus side, I am staying at Joel's tonight while Dad woos his beloved with smooth jazz rhythms and fancy Italian restaurant fare. I have told him to go easy on the cologne, because he never does and I am feeling charitable. He probably intends to make a night of it, judging by the sparkling variety of glasses laid out beside the drinks cabinet, and the fresh lilies in vases in the sitting room and hall. We left very similar lilies on Mum's grave last Sunday. I left a primrose as well. I always do, whenever I can find one. They were her second favourite flower; cowslips were her favourite, but she called me Primrose because, in fairness, who wants to be called Cowslip?

Anyway, Joel's and my plan for tonight is without flaw. His mum bought us cookie mix and ice-cream, so we are going to make cookies and put them in bowls of ice-cream while they're still all yummy and warm. It will be delicious melty goo. We've rented both *Addams Family* movies as well. I'm packing black silky pyjamas with a white cat embroidered on the pocket; it will match the gothy kind of vibe we're going for. I have no desire to be a goth, but I do kind of envy the clothes they wear. It must be really fun to wake up in the morning when you're a goth. Like 'I wonder will my black lace parasol go with my gothic Lolita skirt and Edwardian-style blouse? Yes it will, because luckily they are both also black. Being me is awesome.'

Also, when you're a goth there is no such thing as too much make-up. It really is dreadfully win-win. Maybe I should re-invent myself a bit more completely in honour of secondary school. I'll miss Joel when we're at different schools. But, you know, God forbid he'd make his recently bereaved and closest friend marginally happier by keeping her

company through the hormone-infested hallways of
our secondary school experience. Oh no, not Mr
Selfish Pants. He is moving onto bigger and better
and more masculine things, i.e. the previously
mentioned St John of God's School for Boys. If he
is not careful I will tell everyone there that he sometimes lets me give him face-masks. (St John of God's
is a weird name for a school. I mean, if you're a saint
you kind of have to be 'of God', don't you? I mean
you're hardly St John of Satan, or St John of
Celebrity Dancing on Ice.)

Anyway, I don't want Joel not to be there in my
new secondary school. Who will I hang out with at
break? Who will I make fun of the other kids with?
(The ones who are all about chasing games and
flirting with each other. That became kind of a thing
just before the summer holidays. I can only hope
first year will be less flirty than sixth class. Or *waaay*
more flirty, if it turns out to be full of boys who are
so pretty and mean they could be in films about
motorcycles and doomed love.)

Speaking of flirty, the old man has left out his
guitar on purpose, as a 'talking point'. Oh dear. I will
admit it worked on me, back when I was younger
and he was still an every-second-weekend dad. He
used to learn the themes of my favourite Saturday
morning cartoons and play them for me, before I
grew up a bit and became less easy to delight, and
then ... everything else happened, and I became a

proper burden instead of some sort of exotic pet that he only had to keep amused for two days at a time. But on to bigger, brighter and more delicious things – Joel's mum's car just pulled up, woo!

HEDDA

So, it's a week on and I'm at school. My year is quite small: just twenty two others and not one of them a looker. Boywise, I mean. Some of the girls are terribly pretty even though they have dull, lifeless normal-coloured hair like ordinary folk. I would totally trade in my jet-black locks for a petite yet womanly figure, though. Not that I'm all hulking and masculine like a body-building cage fighter; I'm kind of normal-sized: normal height, normal weight, normal features. On the plus side, my skin is kind of clear, apart from the odd spot. Well, at least my outer beauty does not match my inner beauty, otherwise I'd be in proper trouble, with a nose like my father's and an enormous mouth filled with pointy teeth for snapping at people.

This evening I got to meet my dad's new fancy woman, Hedda. She is not what I expected at all. Not at all like my dad's usual type, which is a porcelain, horsey-looking blonde with a slinky body and a snarky laugh. That's what his previous three girlfriends were like (at least the ones who mattered enough to get an introduction to my good self).

Anyway, Hedda Cabbage (she's nice and all, but a good pun is hard to let go of) doesn't seem like that at all. She's clever and actually kind of human. Which is a good thing because maybe it will rub off on Herr Hairy von Lippenstein. Did you know *croimeal* is the Irish word for moustache? We learned that in school today from our Irish teacher, who is apparently trying to grow one. It really doesn't suit him, but I am probably biased, not being a fan of hair next to my mouth.

First Year, classes-wise, is not too bad. More on that later.

Now, back to the laydee my dad's been romancing (*eww*). I have got to give the man some credit. He does not skimp. No skimping for the daddy man. It's all china plates and hidden takeaway boxes so he can pretend he cooks. He does not cook. I can cook better than he cooks and I'm not allowed near the oven since the great lasagne debacle of last summer. Although I don't know if Mum's rules still hold true now that I'm with Dad. I mean, he doesn't know a lot of them. Something to think about, along with all the other nonsense.

Oh, also, he had this bottle of wine that was, like, older than I am and all dusty and stuff. He told us this back-story about this 'secluded vineyard' he knows somewhere out foreign, where they follow the old traditions and stomp on the grapes in their bare feet to smush them up and get the juice out. I, of

23

course, had to let him know how much I would pay not to have to drink a bottle of sweaty-foot-flavoured beverage, and Hedda let out a roar. I thought she was hurt, but she was laughing her head off and saying 'She's got you there, Fintan.' (She still drank it, though.) Dad laughed right along with us, but his eyebrows were saying, 'You're grounded.' He is *so* two-faced. Bleh.

But Hedda? Well, I like some things about her, which is not to say she won't turn out to be dreadful. I mean, she is seeing my father, after all. But she did call him on his €250 tie made by idiots, for idiots. She was all 'Really, Fintan? On a tie? *Really*?'.

Also, her fashion sense is amazing, all jewel colours and delicate jewellery that complements her skin, which is the colour of milky coffee. (She looks way too exotic and interesting to be Irish, but Irish she is: a Dubliner, born and reared.) Her hair is in all these little plaits and it's really long and shiny. I hope Dad doesn't pull his usual tricks on her, and I don't come home to find her crying in the kitchen some day. I also like that, even though she's nice, she's not like Mum in any way. She's kind of her go-getting, accessorising polar opposite, and she wasn't all patronising and trying to include me just so my dad would see that she was making an effort and stuff. When she did talk to me, it was because she seemed interested, or to make fun of Dad. They have this kind of witty repartee thing going on; I got the feeling

WITTY REPARTEE: Generally amusing exchange of witty remarks. At least, I imagine it's actually supposed to be witty if done properly but when Dad's involved it goes a bit like this: 'Can I steal you away to the sitting room milady?' 'Oh, so you're a thief?' 'Only of *you*.' And then they laugh delightedly. The flower of their youth may be gone but they can still say ridiculous things to each other and pretend they're being all flirtily clever and make innocent thirteen-year-olds blush and feel like they want to leave the room for a bit of a puke. Gah.

that everything is going on between the lines or underneath the surface when they speak. I'm probably too young to understand what is between them, and I'm really glad of that sometimes, because who wants to know that kind of thing when it comes to grown-ups, and if it's bedroom-type stuff, then *ew*. *Ew. Ew ew ew ew ew ew.* Ew to infinity. Ew to the power of ew.

I will definitely stop approving of Hedda if she sleeps over tonight. Because hanging out with the fluffy-lipped fellow of her own free will is creepy enough, but *the other thing?* Evidence that she is one sandwich short of a picnic.

Dad's last girlfriend, Cynthia, used to stay over all the time, even when I was around at weekends, in the old flat. She was a picnic that had no sandwiches at all, although it did come in a very pretty basket, all highlighted hair and bronzed skin. Mum used to

25

hate dropping me off when Cynthia was around, because Cynthia would be all 'I love your top' and fake and even I could tell that she was being insulting and Dad didn't give a hoot. I think he kind of liked it because Mum and him weren't exactly friends, even though they had to get on because of me. Did I mention that Mum is younger than my father? Way younger. Like, fifteen years younger.

Was, I mean. *Was* way younger than Dad. My mother was way younger than my father. Until she died. Does your age change after you die? Do you get older anyway or do you just stay the same? Or are you gone, not any age at all? You always think that older people will die first, like the number of years you've been around is some sort of indicator of how long you've got left. But that's not how it is at all. Anyone can die. I could die tomorrow. Or Joel. Or even Dad.

This next thing is something I feel really guilty about, but I'm going to write it down anyway. I used to wish – actively wish – that Dad had died instead of Mum. I used to beg God. In my head, all the time; I never did out loud. Not that I wanted Dad to die. But I loved Mum more. I needed Mum more. And it might be horribly selfish but I love and need her more even now, and if I could make that swap I would. Because grief counselling and acting out and everything else that's supposed to make me better aren't really going to change anything, are they? I see my life all mapped out in front of me and I do not like it one bit, not at all. Nothing I can do will really change anything.

I have Roderick on my tummy and I'm in my bedroom. He is warm and soft and his little claws are digging through my T-shirt. I don't think rats can cry or know what it means or anything but he's nestling into me and I think he knows I'm sad.

If I die, Roderick will live in Joel's house. I gave him an envelope with that and a list of all the stuff that he can have if I die on it last week when he came over to my house to play Scrabble and watch *Ratatouille*. (I think it's Roderick's favourite film, mostly because it's the only one I specifically move his house in front of the television for.) So me and Joel were sitting at the table, and I had just gotten a triple word score on the word 'evident', and I knew that I had to say it and so I looked down at the floor and explained what was in the note really quickly, and he put it in his bag and promised to keep it safe in a really low, serious voice that's different from his normal one and we were quiet for a bit and then I threw a Scrabble tile at him, and so began the battle to end all battles.

I'm feeling a bit better now. Dad's saying goodbye to Hedda. I can hear the murmur at the door. Once he's in bed I might sneak down for some more of the chocolate cake we had for dessert. It was delicious and just might cheer me up if I have

27

a cup of milk with it. And nobody need ever know – the perfect, tasty crime. *Muahahahahahahahaha!!!*

PROPER BIG GIRL AND BOY SCHOOL, NOW WITH ADDED HOMEWORK!!

..is where I will be returning tomorrow for the fun-filled and exciting week two! It is a bit strange without Joel, but I knew it would be. There are people I talk to in class and stuff, but no one even comes close to Joel. I hope he likes macho, macho school. I still feel a bit sensitive about that because I would have gone anywhere to be with him – well, except, obviously, the place where he ended up going, seeing as how I'd need to get a gender reassignment. But we are still in the same town. (I had a feeling Papa Bear had a few tricks up his sleeve. There were a few boarding school homepages in his internet browser history and I was very close to confronting him, but luckily it didn't end up being a thing.) Anyway, seeing as how he clearly wants to be away from me it is a good

GENDER REASSIGNMENT: Exactly what it says on the tin – giving a girl boy bits or a boy girl bits. This is brilliant if you have been born in the wrong body or yearn for the ease and convenience of the standing-up wee.

thing that I'll be moving on. My life will be changing, hopefully for the better.

Anyway, for English and Religion we have a brand new teacher, Ms Smith, who hasn't been at this school before. She's also our class tutor, which is like a spy for the principal in our classroom and traditionally we are supposed to make her life a misery. I quite like her, though. She's young and has freckles and dark hair with bits of bright red in it and a nose piercing. She looks like she should be a waitress in a cool café or a professional street fighter or something. If our school ever gets attacked by a horde of zombies or a dangerous biker gang, we should be sound as long as we are in English or Religion class at the time. If it is Business Studies or Science we will be almost completely screwed, although I could possibly escape while they feast on the remains of the fragile Sr Gloria who is wispy and probably mostly made of lace. Fingers crossed I won't get on Ms Smith's bad side.

I probably will, though. There's something about me that annoys teachers. Maybe it's because I'm clever and not afraid to speak my mind, or contradict them when they make a mistake, or stand my ground when they think I'm wrong but I know I'm right. If you do that, a lot of them peg you as a troublemaker, like Ms McSpadden did last year, at the beginning of it anyway, though she was nice as pie at the end of it. Being bereaved has a remarkable effect on the way people treat you. I wonder if it would be different if I were a boy instead of a girl. Because I'm not the loudest in the room by a long shot.

I think there's something about an intelligent girl who speaks her mind that really gets people's goats. I don't know why that's even a saying, getting someone's goat. It's not like everyone has their own goat and gets really annoyed when someone tries to get it, possibly with the intention of climbing up on it for an illicit piggyback. Wouldn't that be amazing, though? I'd love a goat. Ever since I read *Heidi* I thought it'd be cool to have one, although maybe one of those little pygmy ones instead of a full-size one. I'd put a pink ribbon with a bell on it around its neck and a silver hoop in its ear (I think it's okay to do that to a goat) and I'd call it Suki or Meiko or something adorable like that. And she would be a disgracefully bold and hoppy little thing, but would sometimes let Roderick travel in a little basket on her back.

NOTES ARE A SCANDAL

This came today:

Mary Immaculate Secondary School

Dear Mr Hamilton,

I would appreciate the opportunity to meet with you concerning Primrose. Would 3pm on Wednesday be convenient for you? Lucrezia Smith, the tutor for 1A, will also be present at the meeting.

Sincerely,

Fatima Cleary

Fatima Cleary
Principal

I haven't done anything. I don't understand. And Triona wants to meet Dad for a 'chat' as well. Agh. This really sucks. Why can't everyone just leave me alone?

LATER ...

I asked around. Turns out all the 'broken' kids in the class got them: Ella, who has autism and needs a helper in the class in case she gets agitated; Caleb, from old school, who was always a bit of a bully but has gotten *waaay* worse since his parents split up; Ciara, although she's pretty normal for someone who enjoys eating her own hair; and Syzmon, who just moved here from Slovakia and doesn't really speak much because his English isn't great. That's quite a little gang actually; maybe I should make them my cohorts. Together we could revolt against the system, storming the streets and yelling *à bas les aristos!* like angry French peasants in some historical drama on Sunday nights on the BBC.

Anyway, Dad is still well annoyed about the note. Who knew parenting would sometimes involve missing an hour or two of work? He works for himself; it's not like his boss is going to get angry at him, because he *is* his boss. And it's not my fault. It's my teacher. I totally haven't done anything even remotely on a par with my hair-eating, kid-hitting co-losers. At least not this year. So far.

MY HERO

We had to do an essay on 'My Hero' for English. Puke. Anyway, I wrote one version of it for fun but handed up some stupidly predictable tripe about Anne Frank, who lived in an enclosed space with family and family friends for a long, long time without killing any of them. Her diary ends with her saying that things would be better if there weren't any other people in the world. Which is kind of what Hitler thought too, only Anne Frank means it differently and kind of in a hopeful, trying-to-be-herself-and-failing-because-of-all-the-disappointment-and-crushing-of-dreams way. Or something. Anyway, I liked that – the way Anne thought, I mean. But not the essay.

33

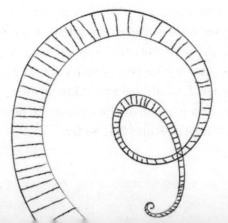

THE ESSAY I DIDN'T HAND UP

By Primrose Leary

My hero is my dad, Fintan Tallulah Hamilton. He is the bee's knees and the pyjamas of the cat. He earns lots of money, even though it is a recession and everything, which is kind of amazing, and he lives in a very expensive house. He will not buy things that are in a sale. His kitchen is full of saucepans that are expensive. He buys them in shops that have doormen. He never cooks, though. My dad has got what he calls 'style'. He is no one's patsy. I do have an Uncle Patsy but my dad does not speak to him because he does not like being reminded that he grew up on a farm. My father will not admit to being of farming stock, except when he feels it would impress people who might give him money. Did I mention he's loaded?

My dad likes things that he can buy. My dad does not like having to fork out for art classes and expensive school uniforms. His priorities are really clear and his moral compass always points to M for money. He does not do stupid things, like forgetting to look before crossing the road, or getting knocked down by a car. He is also stupidly rich. I would like to be just like him when I grow up only without the ridiculous moustache. Go Fintan. Woo.

ANALYSIS

So I told Joel about Dad's meeting with Fatima and Lucrezia. (Maybe the whole meeting business is worth it just to find out what ridiculous first names they both have [says Primrose]. Maybe people named after things you'd find in a meadow shouldn't throw stones.) Anyway, I overheard Dad on the phone to someone, not sure who, but he used the words 'precocity', 'anger' and 'at the end of my tether' so I assume he was talking about *moi*. I think he fears I will ultimately outsmart him and take over his company, just so I could change its name to something ridiculous like No Pants Industries and humiliate him further. Lucky for him I have no desire for a job that involves screaming down the phone at people while dressing in expensive yet boring clothes.

And I felt a little persecuted, so I rang Joel, and we talked about things that had nothing to do with what I was worried about (skull-pattern clothes, the possibility of getting braces and how the colouredy ones freak us out, and who would win in a fight between Iron Man and Wolverine). Then we talked about things Joel was a bit worried about (making friends at his new school, being crap at sport, having next to no interest in being good at sport and whether he should

35

MOI: The same as me, only better, because it is in French and therefore reeks of berets and delicious pastries. Pronounced 'mwah'. French is one of the new subjects that I like, because it reminds me of crusty baguettes and going on my holidays.

get a fringe – he should not). Then we talked about things I was worried about (the meetings, that I'm a bad person and that's why I have so much negativity around me, and the possibility that me and Joel will drift apart and have no time for my girlish dramas now that he's attending Boy Central). He was really good and made me feel loads better, because he'd been worrying about it too – the drifting, not the me being a bad person, which he said was a load of pants. Then Anne called him for dinner and so I reminded him not to get a fringe and hung up. I'm glad to have a friend like that. He's like my brother, only we get on and he's not related to my stupid father.

Recently I have been a bit bold when I visit Triona's house of feelings and acceptance. I've been answering her questions with questions, and not interrupting her stupid meaningful pauses. Because that's how she was getting me. The pauses. I don't like uncomfortable silences. I've been debating taking in a leather-bound notepad of my own and taking notes about her. Like 'has no sense of humour' and 'doesn't take kindly to this sort of thing'. Ha. I probably couldn't get away with that, though. Sigh. Actually, in the last session (I go every Friday, which means I can't take the drama classes I want to go to which would be more fun and also cheaper which is why it is strange that Ebeneezer Hamildad didn't go for them), she did suggest something helpful: writing letters you're never going to send to people just to get your feelings down on paper. But then she suggested some physical activity, like karate or pilates or some other things I really wouldn't be interested in, so I think her whole suggestions thing is pretty hit and miss. Something was bound to interest me at some point.

PRECOCITY: Being too grown-up for your own good. Knowing things early, like how to win an argument with your sorry, moustachioed excuse for a father. People call me precocious and then pat me on the head sometimes, which is really, really patronising and kind of stupid seeing as how I'm all precocious and stuff. Not to be confused with obnoxious, which I am so not.
I am freaking adorable.

OBNOXIOUS: Obnoxious people are the kind of people that make you puke a little in your mouth, not because of something like warts or smelliness, but because of their personalities. Things can be obnoxious too, if they're yucky. Things that are not yucky can be obnoxious too, if they are being flaunted by people who are obnoxious as evidence of how wealthy and successful they are. On the surface, my dad's ties are no more obnoxious than the next old man's. Once you find out what they cost, though, you get small amounts of mouth puke and a general 'what??!!' feeling. This means: 'Congratulations, ties, you have just become obnoxious.'

It's not like I make it easy for her. It's not like there's anything wrong with me that you can put your finger on. I haven't stopped eating or started cutting myself or stealing or anything that you read about girls who are broken on the inside doing in the 'true life' stories in teen magazines. I just grieve and feel so heavy inside or something. Like nothing will be okay, and I'm lazy, very lazy, because even getting out of bed feels like a pointless exercise. I'd rather just flop down on my pillow and wait for the worst. Because it could happen. Because it already has and is and will again. The newspapers, the faces around me just make me feel so lonely and so scared and I wish that Triona could just give me a dog tag or an identity bracelet that could tell people this, like diabetics have, which could warn them off or something. But she can't because it's only feelings. And besides, I don't really tell her all that much.

APRÈS MEETING

So, after chatting to both of the meddling witches, Captain Moustache failed to report back to me:

'How did it go?'

'Fine.'

'*Fine* how?'

'*Fine,* fine. I have some thinking to do now. Go and do your homework or something.'

'Already done. Work thinking or me thinking?'

'*Prim*-rose.'

'*Fin*-tan.'

'For God's sake.'

So I found out nothing, but I am wondering about it. Stupid second-level education. Stupid Mary Immaculate in particular. Hate it. I'm tired and am making little jumpers for Roderick out of odd socks. So far he has a pink and white stripy one with a cupcake on it, which makes him look like the girliest sailor that ever there was, and a red woolly ribbed one for sitting by the fire at Christmas time, toasting marshmallows and laughing wholeheartedly at the sheer joy of it. I don't think you can toast marshmallows on a gas fire. They'd probably taste nasty. And it'll be a cold day in hell before Daddy grass bilong mouth ever takes the time to do something that domestic. For some reason, he does not like me to play with the fire. Because he thinks I'd burn him as boy-witch (warlock?), or something. We read a short story about that kind of thing in English class today. It was really scary, not in that I was scared reading it or anything, but it is really frightening that stuff like that could and did happen. And it still does – not like witch trials, but the not liking of people who are different. I mean, I don't mind being kind of by myself at break now, because I'm not really. I can join in whenever I like because me and the others get on grand on a superficial level and so on.

39

Ciara is going through a bit of a rough patch. She used to be really close with Karen, Joan and Siobhán, but now they're like a little gang of three and all giggly and stuff, and they make little jokes that don't include her and sometimes go off and leave her by herself. She was telling me about it today. I was keeping her company, because she can be all annoying and hair-flicky and 'oh-my-god-a-boy!!' but nobody deserves to feel completely left out. And it's not just at school either. They all live really close to each other, and they've stopped calling over to her house to ask her to come out, and they've been going to town and the cinema without her and not telling her about it till after. No wonder she eats her own hair. Although she kind of always did that – I remember her doing it in baby infants – but, as quirks go, it's somewhere between accidentally spitting on the person you're talking to and public nose-picking – oddly disgusting, as opposed to out and out puke-making. It's strange that she does it and I don't know why she feels the need to do it, because she's such a tall drink of normal in every other way, all pink accessories and fitting in and knowing all the gossip and, what's more, actually caring about the gossip. I don't really understand; I'll never be like that.

I think I'll always be on the outside looking in, but if I was on the inside for more than twenty minutes I'd suffocate and be clawing at the doors and windows to get out.

TWO DECISIONS FROM THE OFFICES OF THE GREAT MOUSTACHE

The first one is that I am being 'minded' after school by Ella-who-got-a-note-as-well's mum, who Dad knows from the golf club, weirdly. She will pick me up after school and I'll go to their house and do my homework and some talking and stuff with Ella until my Dad comes to pick me up after he finishes work.

It's weird. I haven't been minded since I was about eight, although I did hang out at Joel's a lot, instead of heading home to an empty house when I knew Mum would be at work. I was happiest when she was between jobs, because she'd have all this free time and she'd bake and take me places and so on – to stop her getting depressed, she used to say.

But anyway, it'll be all right, I suppose. Ella doesn't talk much, so I'll be mostly left alone to do my homework and watch bad TV. I wonder if they have the channels? I hope their house is big enough for me to do homework and reading and so on by myself, without getting under people's feet. I think Dad's paying her to mind me but I'm not sure because he went on and on about how it would be good for Ella as well, which is total pants because she doesn't even like people all that much. Bleh. He better be paying Mary. And paying her well, because I can be kind of a handful. I'd rather not be there, actually, but I can't be bothered getting all het up about it, because I don't want to give him an excuse to call up Ms Smith or Triona for a 'follow-up meeting'. Which is exactly the sort of greasy, schmoozy thing he'd only love to do, like 'What a good father I'm being,' or 'It's a tough situation, but I'm doing the best I can for Primrose.'

Tough, my foot. My mum had it tough, only she didn't moan about it. She was eighteen when she got pregnant with me – that's only five years older than I am now. AND he was thirty-four at the time, which is seriously creepy. I mean, he would have been fifteen when she was born, the dirty old freak. Ick. I never really thought about it that much before. I mean, Mum never made it into an issue. But I know he did break her heart. I heard her say that to Anne, Joel's mum, one evening when we were playing and they were drinking wine. But anyway, I suppose that's all in the past now. History. But it is *my* history and I'd love to get the answers to the questions that didn't occur to me when she was alive, the questions I'm probably still not old enough to ask and get the full answer to. Because, apparently, in spite of my teenage status and brand new school, I still need to be minded. Humph.

And the other thing is that I am going to spend the bit of Christmas break that comes after Christmas on a farm in Mayo with my uncle Patsy and his wife Éanna, who I've met a grand total of once, when I was two. This is because Dad is taking

> **UNCALLOUSED:** Soft, smooth, without any of the calluses you would get from doing physical work like lifting things or farm work or excessive knitting. Méabh, Mum's friend, has a knitting callus on her index finger that feels harder than the soles of my feet. And I walk around the house barefoot a lot because I can never find both slippers at once, so the soles of my feet are not very soft at all.

Hedda Cauliflower to New York. Roderick is coming with me, so Dad is going to drop me off and pick me up after. He is weirdly agreeable about that, probably because he expected more of a battle. I don't really care. I can be mopey and disagreeable anywhere – it's a talent of mine. He will totally try to back out of giving me a lift down, I know he will. He hasn't been back there in years, because of being a fancy baron of industry who wears cashmere and has the delicate, uncalloused hands of a citified fancy man. Do you know what he actually said to me? 'Hedda was all for taking you with us, but I know you're not ready for that just yet.' Upon which he patted my hand tenderly, like a dad in a TV show.

Um ... *really*? I'm not ready for a week in the city of the apples that are enormous with a woman I don't hate? (And, alright, Dad too but you can't have everything.) But nine days on a farm with an aunt and uncle I haven't seen in a decade is peachy keen and a delightful prospect altogether. Truly my father is a caring and awesome individual. I am blessed to have him. Blessed.

A SILLY THING I DID

Ugh, I'm such a dope. I invited Ciara to the cinema with me and Joel this weekend. He's going to be so annoyed. Not because of the way she eats her hair, but because of how annoying she is in other ways. She was all 'You should really think about getting your roots done' today. Yes, I'll get my roots done and while I'm at it I'll try to remember that I'm not, like, twenty or something. God. Although I do need to do something about the brown top of my head. It is a style that will not be catching on any time soon. Dad won't let me within spitting distance of a hair salon for a good long time, but I could pick up a box of dye and try to do it myself. But that's not the point. Who is she to criticise my hair like some middle-aged woman? I know hers is good enough to eat, but she should leave mine alone. Oh, snap. Which is another annoying thing she says, like if you say something mean about someone, she'll be all 'Oh, snap'.

My time with Joel is limited and precious and she may well ruin it. I am very lucky not to be one of those people who have, like, millions of friends. My head would probably explode from the stress.

44

Anyway, it is Saturday tomorrow, so it will all be over soon. Maybe I should ring Joel and tell him she's coming. Or should I keep it as a delightful surprise? I'm such a mean girl sometimes; why can't I just stop criticising people all the time? In my head, I mean; I don't do it out loud. Well, not constantly.

And Ciara is mostly nice too. She can be really sweet and funny. But why would I say something nice when there's important complaining to be done? Moan, moan, moan. Soon I'll start on the weather and the quality of sleep I get at night and then one horrible morning I'll wake up complete with moustache (boo) and platinum card (yay). Actually, the moustache thing would be pretty funny, but only for, like, a day.

45

OH NO!!!!

Roderick is missing. I was taking a photograph of him prancing about in a very small top hat that once belonged to a Ken doll when he jumped off my bed and ran out the door. In the old house he was always fairly easy to find, because it was a whole lot smaller and I knew all of his favourite haunts – the sofa cushions, behind the computer desk or in the laundry pile – but the new house is huge and unfamiliar to him and he could literally be anywhere. He has been missing for three hours and counting. I am beginning to despair. This will not do at all at all.

I've searched every room in the house (there are fifteen) and closed all the doors and all the windows to prevent him escaping into the big bad world. I've turned off all the appliances as well, so I can hear him scuffling. If he makes so much as a squeak or a chatter I will be on to him and no mistake. I hope I find him before it's time to go to the film cause there's no way I'll be able to concentrate on it or even chat properly to Joel or Ciara at all, knowing he could be anywhere, that once Dad gets back from golf he could collapse onto the sofa and squish Roderick thoroughly and without mercy, or leave the front door open so he can bring in his clubs and other golfish accessories – stupid pants, pointy shoes etc – and let Roderick escape.

I should probably cancel. I'd feel a lot better about it if it was just Joel, but Ciara's a new friend, and she's sensitive. Her feelings might be hurt. I don't know. I miss Roderick, and will not dress him up in novelty costumes any more if only he comes back. Well, I won't do it half as often anyway. He did look amazing in that hat. Like a tiny tap-dancing nobleman.

LATER

The rat has been located. I didn't want to leave until he had been found, captured and secured in his cage, which now has shoelaces holding the door shut in case he has learned to release the catch. So Joel and Ciara ended up coming over here instead, and we all searched the place from top to bottom. (Found an anti-baldness lotion and a tiny safe in Dad's room; he is both pathetic and mysterious, like an obnoxious spy.) Ciara was amazing. She drew up a grid for every room, and once we had finished searching a room we closed the door and checked it off.

Roderick was nestled under the drinks cabinet. I should have suspected as much: he is a rebel and a hedonist. Luckily, he was only delighted to be wooed back into his cage with treats and affection. Fintan, who arrived just before the rat-location, was very relieved. He had been getting up on his high horse about special wires that should remain un-nibbled, and the importance of a house unmarred by small piles of rat poo (as a result of which we did a brief rat-poo hunt – clean as a whistle).

So then Fintan ordered us pizza. Yum, yum. It was really fun, almost like a sleep-over actually, cos Ciara didn't get picked up till ten and Joel stayed even later. It wasn't exactly a wild and crazy rollercoaster ride, but it was really, really pleasant. I like that word; things aren't often pleasant. And I'm glad they got on so well, although Joel did have cause to roll his eyes to heaven when she wanted to watch one of the High School Musicals instead of something with a body count. (Of course, the only high school musical we approve of is *Grease*.)

It just goes to show, there's nothing like a crisis to bring people together, which I said to Fintan as Joel's mum's car sped off into the night. He was all 'And that, Primrose, was nothing like a crisis.' Pah. His brain has been corrupted by share prices and foreign markets. I gave him a little smile that said, 'you poor, foolish, man,' and resolved that next time Roderick 'went missing', he would magically turn up in the sock drawer of a certain vain and selfish golfer, even if he did buy us warm and cheesy food with various toppings.

Oh, I almost forgot: Uncle Patsy rang today. Dad was out but I talked to him for a while. It was mostly awkward, 'How are you getting on?' 'How are *you* getting on?'-type chat, but he did apologise for not making it to Mum's funeral – Éanna was in hospital at the time, having a baby. And – get this – they have a pet fox called Sionnach who lives in their garden and will eat from your hand once he gets to know you. This is both fantastically cool (if by cool I mean kind of nerdy, but I can't help it, I love the idea of seeing a fox at close range who isn't all mangy and going through bins or all grey and smushed into the middle of the road) and worrying: I mean, what if the fox takes a shine to the bold (yet also plump and appetising) Roderick? I hope my room has a lock. But maybe that wouldn't keep him out. Foxes are supposed to be cunning – just look at the simile. It's not 'as cunning as a ... something-

HEDONIST: a shirker of duty and a doer of things that are extremely naughty, in a good way. When Joel goes to the cinema, he mixes his chocolate covered peanuts into his popcorn because he is a hedonist, and cares for naught but gluttonous delights! 'Let the gossips and scandalmongers talk,' he says, 'for they know nothing of my delicious pleasures and dark desires.' I generally remain silent, but express my disapproval by eating about half of this devilish mix. By way of saving him from himself, you understand.

other-than-a-fox'. And Roderick is only small, and to a fox, possibly delicious. Maybe I better leave him with Joel. But I don't want to do that either.

The new baby's name is Phineas. Isn't that weird? It's so not the name of a baby; it's the name of a bearded and obnoxious druid who hangs around oak forests knowing things and possibly playing the harp. Foxes and babies and uncles, oh my!

49

A POEM I WROTE

We had to write a poem for English, about animals. It is supposed to be 'in response' to some stupid poem we read about a rabbit being worried in a snare. I had a few false starts like,

Oh noes said the rabbit
I'm trapped in a snare
I wish I was bigger
the size of a hare

then I'd chew through the wire
that's eating my paw
and kick it to bits
with my awesome hare claw
but I live in a world
where rabbits are weak
and so I will stay here
and try not to freak
about all of the squeezing
that causes me pain
as if I were a man
who was hit by a train.

I am clearly a lyrical genius, fighting her way up through the streets and hallways of Mary Immaculate Secondary School, only with rhymes and imagery as my gun and highly essential second gun. All the girls want to be me; all the boys want to date me. It's hard out there for a pimp.

This is the one I actually ended up using. It is clearly in honour of my magnificent escaping possible fox-dinner, Roderick:

In Praise of Rats

Tigers roar,
Bats flap,

Sloths snore,
Cats nap,
Puppies yip,
Rabbits hop,
Foxes nip,
Fish flop,
Cows chew,
Hippos drool,
Dogs poo,
Rats rule!

FELIX THE NOT-CAT

51

I'm in a boy's room – a *proper* boy, not just Joel. It's less interesting than it sounds, though. Ella has an older brother, Felix, and his room is where I get to do my homework. He has a desk and doesn't get back from after-school study until a quarter past six (he's in Junior Cert year.) He has a part-time job in a café at the weekends as well. That's cracked. That's, like, almost as many hours as my dad works, and he's always getting called a workaholic, except by me – I sometimes call him a lazy good-for-nothing slacker, and tell him my friends' dads all work ninety-hour weeks, just to be the voice of dissonance. That's one of my new vocabulary phrases. Ms Smith makes each of us write the new words and sayings we come across in a little notebook, which she calls our personal dictionary. This is so that we will not freak out next year when we are confronted by Shakespeare and all his yons and hithers. Syzmon's forever writing in his one; he'll probably have volumes by the end of the year. So far, I've only got five entries:

PARIAH: A loser, loner-type who is shunned and made an example of by the people around her. Or him. But historically? Usually her.

PREPOSSESSING: The new 'hot'; appealing and attractive.

AVANT-GARDE: Cool, but also original and different. What hipsters want to be.

YELLOW-BELLIED: Cowardly, but cowardly the way a cowboy or a soldier would say it.

THE VOICE OF DISSONANCE: The one that there always is. The one who doesn't agree with what everyone else agrees with. Tends to annoy people who are not the voice of dissonance.

Anyway, Felix's room is kind of great. It's the polar opposite to mine. Not a floral stencil or a patchwork quilt in sight. It's all black sheets and posters with bands and films on them: Nirvana (Mum loved them too, me not so much, bit moany. I like inner turmoil that I can dance to), My Chemical Romance (blergh – oh, Felix!). Then there's *The Nightmare Before Christmas* (yay!). There's also a skinny, tall poster of a skinny, tall girl in a leather catsuit pouting vampirically. Eep. You don't get many leather-panted vixens round these parts, Felix, but you just keep on hoping. Attaboy. I hope my boobs don't get that big – not very likely, let's face it. But it would be difficult to stand up straight, much less run around on a freezing cold hockey pitch for fifty minutes every Tuesday. It's kind of difficult to run around on a freezing cold hockey pitch no matter what size your breasts are, though.

The word breasts kind of creeps me out a bit, although not half as much as Ms Molloy telling us to be sure to wear dark-coloured knickers under our teeny tiny hockey skirts on match days. I wasn't planning on playing any matches, but I definitely won't be now. Shudder. Maybe it was a nefarious plot to weed out the less than dedicated? You have to be really sporty/body-confident to commit to the twice-monthly bare legged panty-flashing that being on the team would involve. Are boys allowed to come to the games? Because that would be kind of exploitative and pervy.

I feel like I kind of know Felix a bit already. This might be weird, but I love poking around other people's rooms. If I wasn't worried Mary (Ella's mother) would come up and check on me, I'd totally have a rummage through his drawers too. I can't help being curious. I don't have any older brothers to spy on. This could be my only chance to gather intelligence on boy-kind. I've been in Joel's room plenty of times, but he doesn't really count, because he's like me only with boy-parts instead of girl-parts. NOT that I'm thinking about anybody's parts. *Eek*.

Junior Cert books look really hard. Well, the maths ones do anyway. They're all thick and wordy. Perhaps my days of being too clever for my own good are numbered. Once this year is over, I may have to hand in my clogs. I hope not. I know sometimes it is frustrating and makes me feel sad/different/freakish somehow, but I'd way rather be the way I am than not be clever enough for my own good.

I'd say Mary tidied this room before I came over. Nobody keeps their room this tidy all by themselves. My floor at home always has socks and the odd knicker or two lurking somewhere. The last time I tidied it was when Roderick went missing, and that was only so he'd have nowhere to hide.

I'm finished all my work; we only got a bit today. I'm still going to spend as long as I can up here 'doing my homework' because if I go downstairs I'll have to do the awkward chatting thing, and I did enough of that today. Ciara's all buddy-buddy now, she kind of talks at me all the time and my head is officially quasi-wrecked. Plus the three witches decided they don't really like me either and started a rumour that I wet the bed ever since my mum died. Oh, please. I'm ignoring them so they'll go away, but I don't know if that works.

And for the record, it's SO not true. I haven't wet the bed since I was seven and had a dream about swimming in a nice, warm fountain. I was under-standably embarassed, but Mum was great, all clean pyjamas and cuddling me in her bed until I fell asleep, even though it was ridiculously disgusting.

Anyways, if I head downstairs, there's a huge chance that I'll end up keeping Ella company. Not that she's not lovely – she's grand and stuff, but it's hard to have a proper conversation or even just hang out with her because she's the way she is. She doesn't *get* things. Like, I said 'That's cool' to Mary about doing my homework in Felix's room, and Ella told me it was warm, actually, that she didn't need a jacket. Eep. And it makes me feel awkward, like I'm a bad person for feeling weirded out when she goes a bit loopy and starts repeating things or gesturing strangely.

I should go downstairs and hang out with her for a while. I will. In a minute. Or two. Or, like, seven. Seven seems like a good number.

55

QUASI-X: A bit X, kind of X, sort of X, half X. Like Ciara is quasi-annoying, or Fintan's moustache is quasi-ridiculous.

NEFARIOUS: devilish, dastardly and altogether dreadful, e.g. 'The nefarious plan involved ropes, strychnine and the utmost secrecy.' 'Stranger Danger!!!' is what you should scream when faced with a nefarious type of person, driving past and offering sweets and puppies while twirling their moustaches in an abominable manner. I have never yet heard anyone scream 'stranger danger!!!' so either nefarious people are rarer than you'd think, or people do not like shouting ridiculous slogans, even when they apply to the situation in hand.

TALES FROM THE CRYPT

Today was a really strange day. It was really sunny, so during religion class, we went to this old graveyard behind the school to take rubbings of the tombs and gravestones. We each had to pick a grave, take a rubbing of it with a crayon (mine was a bright and perky orange – we didn't get to choose) and then write a diary entry based on that person, the time in which they lived, the age at which they died and so on. I picked Marguerite 'known as Daisy' Mooney who died in 1896, at the age of sixteen. I don't know if I can get into the mindset of someone who actually chose (I assume) to be named after a wildflower.

We don't really have control over our nicknames, though – at least I don't: Joel calls me Prim, Dad calls me Rosie. I have many aliases, like a superhero or a glamorous spy. Mum used to call me Prim and Proper, or Primrosey Primposey, or Pose, or Poser, or Young Lady when she was giving out. She was never very good at giving out or at choosing a nickname and sticking to it.

I wonder what Daisy will be like – the way I write her, I mean. I don't know a lot about 1896. I don't know a lot about now, stuff that is going on in the world at the moment. I mean, I hear the news the odd time, and if someone is robbed, hurt, attacked or killed somewhere nearby (not that anyone's been killed close to where I live, as far as I know), everyone's all talk, and 'isn't it terrible?' But, like, people get killed every day, from all kinds of things – stupid things like hunger and disease and drowning as well as fast-paced action movie things like bombs, car crashes and exploding speedboats. I mean, Mum was just cycling home from work when that drunk guy mowed her down. At least there were no drunk drivers in 1896. Although they did have carriages, so there might have been. I, for one, would not like to be trampled by a team of horses. Maybe that's what I'll say happened to poor Daisy.

Like:

Dear Diary,

Yea, verily I do wish that some kind soul would invent the safe cross code, for deeply do I feel its lack.

Okay, that idea is seriously stupid. But it is kind of an interesting project. It also makes me suspicious that Lucrezia Smith might be a bit of a goth, at least when she's not busy being a teacher.

TOP 10 REASONS LUCREZIA SMITH MIGHT BE A GOTH IN HER FREE TIME.

1 She has multiple piercings.

2 ... and is never without eyeliner.

3 She would not look out of place in a Marilyn Manson video, given proper attire.

4 She wears a lot of black.

5 Her name is Lucrezia, which is so grim it might as well be Morningstar Deathraven.

6   She's kind of cool. Which I also think about the goths that hang around the square in town.

7   Her hair is very, very, very dark brown with red bits. Darkness and blood. Gloom and doom.

8   She took us to a freaking graveyard by way of a lesson.

9   She did that thing about witches in English.

10   She has a really quiet, scary giving-out voice. Caleb found that out the hard way, when he tried to Tipp-ex messages of swear onto one of the headstones. That boy has serious problems. *I* found out the easier way: by eavesdropping on their conversation.

ONE AND A HALF REASONS I MIGHT BE MISTAKEN ABOUT MS SMITH

1   Her name is Lucrezia. If your parents call you that, you can be pretty sure they want you to have gothic tendencies – or at least be a bit pagany. And who wants to make their parents *that* happy?

1.5   She's a religion teacher. I mean, come on.

CRYPT-IC STORIES

Dear Diary,

It is cold here in 1896. In the ground, I mean. I do not think I'm dead. I don't feel dead. Please let me out. Please, someone, let me out.

Daisy

I'm reading a book of Scottish ghost stories that Joel got me when he was in Edinburgh on holidays with his parents. Back in the day, there was an epidemic of grave-robbing in Scotland. And there was a wealthy man whose wife had passed away. In life, she had always worn a ruby ring, so he decided that she would be buried with it on her finger. You can probably see where this is going. The wife was buried in a churchyard, or kirkyard, which I assume is the same as a graveyard. Two criminals heard tell of this ruby ring and, being criminals, they snuck into the cemetary with spades and so on and dug her up. Once they had prised the coffin open, they saw the ring glinting on her finger. It was all they had hoped it would be (fancy and expensive looking), but it soon became obvious that there was a problem. Try as they might, the two grave robbers couldn't prise the ring off her finger. (They should have brought hand lotion or butter. Even I know that. Silly men.)

Eventually they decided the most sensible thing to do was to cut her finger off. I mean, she didn't need it any more than she did the ring, right? So they got out a sharp little knife and set about sawing her ring finger off. I imagine it took a while. And just when they had snapped the finger with its jewel off her, her eyes flicked open. She had been in a coma, unconscious. The shock of pain was enough to snap her awake. She was never really dead at all and had been buried alive. The story finished just as she awoke, but I imagine the aftermath would have been even more horrible. What were they to do? They could hardly put her back where they had found her, at least not without killing her first. And how could she go back, one finger missing and mostly dead, to the husband and the children who had put her in the ground? Does that stuff really happen? Could it happen nowadays when we know so much more stuff? How lonely you would feel. So abandoned by the world.

Mum had a closed casket. Because of the way her body was. The state that it was in. I had a peek, though. I mean, I couldn't not. She was my mum. And even though it was horrible, at least I'm sure that she was dead when she went in the ground. She

61

couldn't look the way she did and be alive. Is that a comfort? Maybe. I don't know. Not really. Not at all. Wow, I'm in a bit of a grim mood. Maybe it's the time of year. Hallowe'en is coming soon, and all.

THINGS THAT HAPPENED IN

First electric trams ran in the streets of Dublin. Wish they were still around; they looked waaay cooler than the Luas. Although, not in Daisy's opinion, as she would never have seen a Luas, because they were not around in 1896, obviously enough.

Ireland's first cinema shows held in Dublin. Black and white, without speaking bits, I assume. I'd probably rather have seen a play, which is an opinion Daisy could totally share ... hmm. I like going to plays, because it feels more special than going to a movie, everyone's all in the same room and there's the sense that something could go wrong, which makes it more exciting. I don't know how people remember all their lines. I have trouble remembering poems and song lyrics, not while I'm by myself, but on the spot in class. Eek. They probably would have had a lot of what Dad calls rote learning, chanting and stuff, when Daisy was at school, but ...

Children would have left school at twelve to start work which sounds quite pleasant but is, in all actuality, eeky, as Daisy would not have been able to spend her money on music and books and clothes because she would have had to give all her money to her parents until she got married and had to give everything she owned to her husband who could lock her up and even beat her if he wanted. But only with a stick no wider than his thumb. Because beating your wife with a stick that's bigger than your thumb is just silliness. I don't know what the powers that used-to-be thought of regular old fist punchings. I'd imagine they were grand.

63

Women were not allowed to vote. Daisy probably wouldn't have been allowed to for another twenty years or so. Only men were allowed to back then, because everyone thought they were cleverer and better able to decide things than women were. Yuck. Women were complaining about not getting votes when Daisy was alive. They were called suffragettes, but most people thought they were a bit daft, and should be given a sound thumb-sticking, at the beginning anyway.

Ireland was still a part of Britain, and would be for like aaaages, till the twenties or something. So Daisy totally missed out on loads of fighting, and an 'epic chapter in our nation's history'. Hmm. I wish I knew when she died, like the month; her gravestone doesn't say. Because I'm not sure what she would have known about or not known about. I wonder if she had a boyfriend. People got married younger in those days, and if they wanted babies they had to get married, or they'd be in terrible trouble because people would think they were all sinful and bold. I probably wouldn't have had a great time of it back then, because of the whole parents not being married thing. Although it'd nearly be worse if they were married, eek. It would have been really shouty and awkward. Because he'd probably still have had girlfriends and Mum would probably still have had a healthy dislike for him. We would have had to escape his clutches, possibly on the brand new electric tram. Convenient!

Underwear was complicated. More complicated than the bras of today, which are still pretty complicated, at least the underwirey ones with gel inserts and removable straps that Mum used to wear on special occasions. They

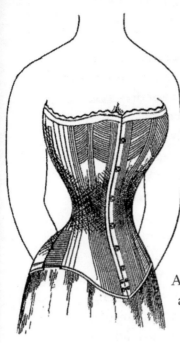

had corsets and petticoats and things called stays – I have no idea what they are. Maybe they make something stay up, like stockings? Also, no tights in 1896. Must have taken *aaaaages* to get dressed.

ELLA AND I

Almost on holidays, woo! Last day at Ella's for a while, I think. She is a strange one; she's on new medication now, but I don't know if it's good. She just seems really tired and dull. Mary told me about it, because I kept asking if Ella was okay; she was so quiet and starey. They want to start her on it when it's almost mid-term so they can keep an eye on her or something. I didn't really understand but it must suck to have to take medication all the time, not just when you're feeling sick, but because of who you are inside, how your brain is made or something. I don't really know what causes it or anything. She thinks about different things to me. I mean, so does Ciara, but Ella thinks in a really, *really* different way and gets het up and angry sometimes, too. She can't even be in the class all day; her helper has to take her out different places. She had a helper, Breege, up until this year but now that Ella's in Mary Immaculate, Breege is gone and there's Maugie, who isn't as good with her. Or doesn't seem to be anyway; Ella seems to be more agitated and nervous in class than she was before.

Although the same goes for me, and for Ciara too, come to think of it. Maybe we're just growing up and not doing it too well. Also, some of the new subjects are kind of stupid – like Civics and Business Studies. On the plus side, *now* I know I never want to be an accountant (*quelle surprise*) or use my right to vote (suck it, suffragettes) unless it's some kind of vote against learning about the voting system which will apparently come up on our Christmas tests.

Ella asked me yesterday why Ciara eats her hair. We were watching TV, and she was drawing in the sketchbook that she always has beside her. I answered that I didn't really know, but I would ask her. Ella said that she doesn't think hair tastes very nice at all. I said I didn't either. That's the kind of conversation we have, short and a bit weird. She's a good person, though, I think. She watches certain things very closely, like animals, then she draws them in her book. I asked her if she would draw me a picture of Roderick, but she has to see him before she can agree. I don't know why; it's not like the other animals she draws are all interviewed and selected after a lengthy process of hemming and hawing and deciding. Or maybe they are; who knows what goes on in her head?

I wonder if I should dress Roderick up in a bowtie and suchlike to impress her. I'll definitely clean out his cage the night before. Odd or normal, no one likes the smell of rat wee and poo to boot. If only he could use a tiny toilet. That would be both handy and adorable. But I would love a portrait of him, especially if I could convince her to put him in a smoking jacket with a pipe in one hand and a fine glass of brandy in the other, as though he were a member of an exclusive gentleman's club like in *Around the World in 80 Days*.

Anyway, a portrait would be really in keeping with the fancy old-fashionedy vibe of my room. I could show it off to people, like a shabby aristocrat pining for the good old days. Only my good old days involve being a lot poorer. Also, I don't think I have the dignity and poise required to be an aristocrat. I'm always bumping into things like coffee tables and postboxes, and knocking things over like jars full of pencils and cups of coffee. Bet Dad regrets getting that cream carpet now. Maybe not as much as he regrets knocking Mum up all those years ago. Why is it that when parents reminisce about stuff it's always about

ARISTOCRAT: Like the cats in the Disney movie The Aristocats, only people. Moneyed, privileged, born-into-good-families people, who often inherit fancy castle-type houses.

how hard they worked and the places they had to walk without shoes and the toys they didn't have. They never say, 'When I was your age I was always stealing things and teasing vulnerable baby animals with sticks.' Which, I bet, was what Fintan was like as a child. It's a little bit what he's like now.

He has a bullying, scary phone voice that he uses for giving out to people at the office. Also quite a wild and cursey vocabulary. He'd make a sailor in an eighteens movie about cursing blush when he's on form. I'd love to introduce angry Dad to Ella when she's in one of her repeaty moods. Hilarity would totally ensue. Well, swearing anyway. Possibly at *moi*.

SPOOKY SPOOKY GHOST NIGHT APPROACHES, ALL MENACING AND FULL OF SWEETS ...

I don't think I'll dress up this year, although I will probably end up putting on some sort of ridiculous nose or hat, just to be 'festive'. It's weird, because Karen and them think dressing up is really 'childish'. Um ... I don't think you're allowed to use that word in such a partronise-y manner while you're still technically a child. Karen's thirteenth birthday's not till December. She does wear a bra, though, so she has the advantage there. Since I became friends with Ciara I have been learning many facts about her ex-friends. She dwells a lot. And by dwells, I mean moans.

Funnily enough, once you're a bit older, dressing up becomes cool again, at least if my mum and her friends were anything to go by. When I was little, Mum used to always throw a fancy-dress party on Hallowe'en night. Loads of people would come and dance and drink her homemade spiced punch that smelled like nail-polish remover. I was always allowed to stay up really late those nights, way after bedtime, and everyone would laugh and chat and make sure I had fun. It was lovely.

I don't see Mum's friends much any more. They were at her month's mind, but now that I live in a different place it's not like they can pop round. Dad wouldn't exactly make them feel welcome. I get texts from some of them sometimes, asking how I am, or remembering little things: a top Sheila forgot to return, Dave asking if Roderick would like some extra rat food he can't get rid of. That kind of thing. But when I lived with Mum, there was always someone popping round for a chat. Our home was always busy, and I miss that a bit. Okay, a lot.

GROWING PAIN(IN THE NECK)S

So, tomorrow is All Hallow's Eve. Not exactly sure what the plan is, but I think Joel and me and Ciara and Joel's friend Liam from school are going to have a scary movie night. Nothing too scary (although Joel is hoping to sneak a couple of fifteens DVDs past his mother and the man in the rental shop. I wish him good luck). I was thinking about maybe dressing all in black and wearing loads of eyeliner as a kind of a tribute to the night that's in it, but not exactly dressing-up dressing up, if you get my drift. No werewolf fangs and stick-on fur for me this year. No fake blood and torn clothes. No cardboard boxes painted to look like a packet of skittles. Bah.

Roll on being older. I really like dressing up. But only when everyone else does too. I'm thinking of having Ciara sleep over some night during the break; I need to talk to her about something. Some*things* actually.

Boobs.

I *finally* need to get me one of those bra things. I've gotten a little, um, pointy recently; it's kind of

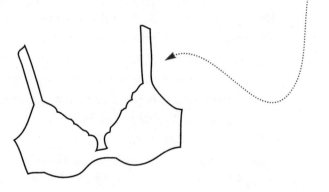

embarrassing and sometimes quite sore. And I can't really talk to Dad about it because of the shame. And also, he'd be all thrilled that I felt comfortable enough to 'confide' in him, and not realise that it was a last resort. Shudder. Also my chestal pokeage is NONE OF HIS BUSINESS. Ugh, even the thought of the awkward hell that the 'little chat' would involve is giving me goosebumps and tummy pains. I'd rather lick chewing gum off the footpath. Anyway, it is baggy T-shirts to the power of loads until I've got a bra or some kind of magical ointment that makes them go away. It would come in a round tub and have a catchy and embarassing name.

REGRETS

I have made a big mistake. Trying to fashion a makeshift bra out of toilet paper and duct tape was utterly, devastatingly, shamefully not clever. And now? It won't come off. It just won't budge; it's like the stickiest bandages of all, the ones you get at the hospital after they take blood that leave a mark on the inside of your elbow and stay put for days. Except instead of my elbow it's most of my upper body. And instead of a teeny, tiny bandage? Oh, God. I wonder if it is possible to actually die from embarrassment. Probably not. Pity.

RELIEF!

It came off after shower number four. Dad began knocking after shower number two, which is also when the hot water ran out. I was all 'Leave me alone!' and 'I'm fine'.

I am cold and embarrassed and still a little bit sticky. This is the scariest Hallowe'en ever, and it's only just after midnight. No one must ever know of my shame. Ever. Roderick is looking at me all smirky. Thank God he can't talk and therefore gossip or mock.

HORROR OF HORRORS

I'm not talking to Joel for the first time ever. I don't think we have ever rowed before and it's killing me because he is the one I chat to about everything and I really want to chat to him about this but I can't because I am not speaking to him because he is a liar and a manipulating bloom of pond-scum. Did I mention I'm angry? I am furious.

So last night, everything was going okay; we were watching a film about flesh-eating zombies that will probably give me nightmares for weeks but was also hilarious and totally worth it. And I noticed Joel was sitting beside me quite pointedly throughout the evening and it never occurred to me that it was because he is the sleazy Lord of Lies; I thought it was because he was my friend and was trying to sit in the middle to make everyone feel comfortable. Not so.

And there was a bit that involved lots of gross guts and inner tummy bits coming out and it was the most disgusting thing I had ever seen (on TV) and it reminded me of something I didn't want to remember, so I got all frightened and shaky, and he was all rubbing my arm and giving me a hug. Not run of the mill, but okay, fine. Comforting.

And then we were putting moustaches on Joel's friend Liam and taking pictures, and that was funny, and we all put fake moustaches on, even Ciara, who came dressed as a fairy. And we were taking pictures of ourselves and of Liam and it was all comedy gold and a bit of a laugh, etc. etc.

And THEN, Joel asks Liam to take a picture of him and me, and even THAT uncharacteristic show of clingy friendship doesn't make me at all suspish. Because I trust Joel not to be a lying piece of poo. And he mutters in my ear, 'Just go along with this,' and then just as Liam is clicking away happily, he kisses me on the mouth. Ew. *Ew. Ew!*

And because I am a friend of friends, I play along nicely and only worry a little bit about all the boy germs that I have just ingested. (There was no tongueage or anything, otherwise I would be writing this from prison where I would be for killing Joel until he was good and dead.) And Ciara was all '*Squeak!*' and 'I didn't know you guys were together.' And Joel was all, 'Really? Well, I suppose it is fairly recent,' and she looked at me all hurt, like, 'Why have you not told me this delectable piece of gossip that I could have spent many's the lunchtime questioning you about?'

Ciara can be a wee bit boy-crazy. Not about real boys, but about the idea of 'having a boyfriend' and 'holding hands' and 'going out'. She reads too many teen mags. So I am smiling through my teeth for *aaaages* until my cheeks are sore and my teeth are wearing down to pointy little nubs from inadvertent grinding. And THEN we watch a vampire film, and Joel has his arm around me, and thank goodness he doesn't go kissing me again, probably because he's as grossed out by the idea as I am. Joel has never really talked about girls (or anyone at all) in a likey kind of way. I suppose I thought we were above that messy, complicated stuff. But maybe he just didn't want to talk about it with me because he thought it would make me uncomfortable or jealous because we are so close. Or were, anyway. Once again, he is a pig of pigs.

And finally when Liam and Ciara (who texted me, like, fifteen times after she left to be all, like, 'oooooh') got picked up, I turn to him and ask what, in the name of all that's awesome, he thought he was playing at? And he was all, 'I've told everyone in school that you're my girlfriend and I needed to prove it. Thanks for being a pal.'

So I replied to this amazing piece of idiocy with a simple, 'And why, for the love of zombie, would you want them to think that?'

And he wouldn't explain.

And I called him a liar.

And he said he was sorry.

And I was, like, 'Ewww'.

And he was, like, 'I know'.

And I was, like, 'Excuse me?'

And then he said it was like kissing a bullfrog.

And I said (and this is probably what made him get nasty; it's kind of a sensitive thing) that I didn't think that he wanted to be kissing anyone just yet, and that even if he was kissing someone, I had always kind of assumed that it would be a boy and not a girl (Kevin from playschool all grown up, perhaps?).

And then he called me a few horrible names and then I called him a lot of horrible names.

And then he got even angrier and said some really nasty, vicious things I can't forget. Like that I was a selfish, superior little princess.

And someone who thinks only about herself since her mother died.

And that sometimes he wondered why we were even friends at all.

So then I called Dad, who was on a date with Hedda, to get him to bring me home. And I picked up my stuff and locked myself in the downstairs bathroom, humming showtunes with my fingers in my ears until Dad called to say he was outside. And Dad was all 'What's wrong love?' but I was too upset to say anything, and besides, it's none of his beeswax. But I was very sad indeed, so we stopped for ice-cream and a chat. Not about Joel being a kiss-stealing liar and a sayer of horrible things, but about zombie films. Dad likes them too (who knew?) and he was very proud that I had sat through the whole thing without wussing out or turning on the lights. When we got home we practised our zombie shuffles getting ready for bed. He looked awful silly, especially when he was brushing his teeth. But he was kind of fun. I wish I could get on with everyone at the same time.

Joel hasn't texted. He is mean. I don't know what's going to happen. I might never speak to him again. And he has loads of my books and some of my fake moustaches. I'd talk to Ciara about it but I don't want to be disloyal. But how can you be disloyal to someone who is so mean? And why is he my best friend and then not acting like a friend at all, but a manipulator and all round sod of turf? This is complicated. If going to secondary school makes people like this, I don't know if I want to go at all any more. I will return to old school, staying in sixth class till I'm twenty-five and utterly disgracing my family. On the plus side, no one will ever be short of things to stick on the fridge. Oh, this is rotten. I'll never get to sleep.

SOD OF TURF: Something brown and smelly that comes from the depths of the earth and should be thrown on the fire because that's all it is good for.

MANIPULATOR: Someone who can get people to do what they want, and not in a good way. In a using people way, like making them his ridiculous puppets that he can make to do whatever he wants. For example if he wanted to pretend one of them was his puppet-girlfriend, a manipulator would have no problem doing just that. Also they wear too much gross boy-deodorant, or maybe that's just Joel.

77

THE PERFECT CRIME

Well, not a crime really. But bold, certainly, and if Dad found out about it he would probably put his angry face severely on. It's about Triona. I have decided that I am a self-actualised and perfectly adorable human being and do not need her sage advice any more. So I rang her up to cancel. I said 'Dad wants me to ring myself because it's my responsibility.' (Smart, huh?) And then I ripped up the cheque into little pieces and went for the yummiest hot chocolate known to man in Café Crème.

SAGE: As wise as an elderly owl, with greying feathers and a degree in astro-physics from a university so exclusive only really really clever people know about it.

I used to go there with Mum all the time for rewards, when I'd gotten ten out of ten on a spelling test (we never get spelling tests here, I think they just assume we can spell everything) or an A in a proper test, or she'd broken up with one of her boyfriends and deserved delicious comfort. I brought my book (re-reading the last few Harry Potters) and sat there for the hour. It was lovely.

The waitress asked for Mum – she didn't know. I don't know why but I said that she was fine and she had gone back to college and was really busy with essays and working. And also that we were going to France for Christmas. I don't know why I lied, but for that hour in the café, I felt like it was true. And it was ten million billion times better than sitting in that dull room of Triona's, feeling like a right moaner and going on about all the things that make me want to scream. Also I would have ended up talking about Joel, who still hasn't rung me (bah), and that is really none of her business. Not that any of it is her business. Stupid Triona, with her deep, calm voice and her slight moustache. But I liked today; I actually felt quite relaxed and happy for a bit; independent. And not a burden on anyone, just a girl drinking a gooey melty cup of yum.

DEVELOPMENTS AND FORMER POSSIBLE PARTY NOSTALGIA

> **NOSTALGIA:** What older people have about the 'good old days'. What sensible people have about sweets that aren't in shops any more, or TV shows that were really good when you were small, but you can't find them on any channel now. Kind of a whiny remembering of better days, like 'Oh, we were happy then.'

Hedda the union is meeting me in town tomorrow. We are going bra shopping! This is weird because it means that a decision was made that I need a bra and that Hedda, and not Dad, should go with me to buy it. Hedda and Dad were talking about my boobs. Eek!

It is going to be embarrassing, but not as embarrassing as it would be if I had to go with Dad.

I rang Ciara today for, like, an hour. We talked about Joel. She said I should have exposed him as the dirty liar he is at the time, and let him deal with the consequences of his actions. She also called him a kiss-rapist (I wouldn't go that far, Ciara). And then she asked me if I thought he was cute. I do not. I mean, he's not bad looking, but I don't, like, *like* him at all. Ciara thinks everyone is cute, though, even Syzmon, who has 'nice eyes' and Caleb who 'has that whole mean and moody thing going on'. Um, creepy much?! Sometimes I worry for her sanity.

I was telling her about going bra shopping with Hedda State, and she said she didn't have to go at all. Her mum works in a shop and measured her at home and got stuff for her and put them in her drawer. I like that; it's so simple. I know Mum would have probably made a big deal of my first bra if she was still around. She was always celebrating little things like that. Like when I passed my piano exams, she baked cupcakes and iced music notes into the top of them. Although I would have been just fine and dandy without an appropriately-shaped cake for *this* particular occasion.

BRA, BRA EILE

... is the name of the shop that Hedda Celery took me to. It was full of lacy sophistication and matching things. I didn't know that your bra was supposed to

SOPHISTICATION: A kind of expensive classiness. People who have manicures that look like real nails only shinier and never seem to get chipped and who know about expensive things and the ways of the world have sophistication. People who have their nails painted bright pink with little butterflies in them do not have sophistication.

They do, however, have amazing nails.

match your undies. Mum's didn't, but I didn't let on when I asked Hedda about it, because I didn't want to let the side down. I am a 30B, which is big for my age, apparently. Although I don't think they get many of my kind in that shop, it seemed to be all women who looked expensive and had very shiny hair. So anyway, Hedda got Saoirse, the owner, who is also her friend from secondary school (nice to know some friendships can last – stupid Joel), to measure my chest, just under my boobal area and then around my bust as well. Very scientific it was too; I was much impressed.

And then I got two white bras, two grey bras (apparently the white bras will also turn grey eventually, but the grey bras will just stay grey and are therefore an awesome idea), one black-and-white spotted bra and one pink-and-white striped bra. The pretty patterned ones also have undies to match. I will feel all secretly fancy when I wear them. They cost LOADS. Hedda whipped out her credit card and was all, like, 'Your dad gave me money for them but I think this is women's business so I'll get these and then we'll go and spend his cash on something fun.'

Something fun was lunch and ice-cream and then clothes! Hedda's only rule was 'no black'. Apparently

> **BUST:**
> A statue of someone's head. Also a lady's chestal region. Which could lead to all kinds of comedic misunderstandings. Eep.

81

I've been wearing black every time she's seen me. I got a purple and grey striped dress, a T-shirt with an evil cat on it, a pair of bright blue trousers, a swirly blue and red skirt and two soft jumpers the colour of jewels. I was all 'Thanks, Hedda!' and she was all 'Thank you *Fintan*,' and we cackled like witches and then bought shoes. This was great because I only have my school ones and my runners – my feet grew this year and those two pairs are all that fit me. Not any more. I got flat petrol-coloured pumps with a white felt rat on them. They were on sale, so they were only, like, ten euro! I can't believe that – who wouldn't want a lovely rat on their shoes? Hedda went Hedda shopping too and bought a scarf with silver and blue thread through it and some shirts that looked boring to me, but she was all 'for work'. We were really tired after our day of spend.

On the way back home, I talked about Daisy. I have four days left to do the essay on her. Hedda told me that there were some black people in Dublin in 1896, but that they would have mainly worked for rich people instead of going to balls and doing fun stuff. I don't think Daisy was rich but Hedda said that she must have had some money if she had a headstone that was engraved and every-thing. Which is nice, because I don't like to think of her being in a workhouse, which is where the really poor people got sent, the ones who had no money at all. We talked about the potato famine as well, because Daisy's parents would have probably been born just after it, so her grandparents would remember it, if they were still alive. I don't have any grandparents left, which is a pity. Hedda has a grandmother still alive who rings her to give out to her every other week. She said this in a nice way, as if she doesn't really mind the giving out.

When we got home, Dad was there, and he'd rented three films, so we could take our pick. We watched one about a girl who could turn into a dog and kept getting into embarassing situations. It was pretty good. Dad was going to phone for pizza, but Hedda called that 'a waste of a lovely kitchen' and made him help her make dinner (cheesy pasta with veg). They had wine; I had coke. Then I went to bed while they watched film number two.

I stayed up for ages sorting my new stuff and reading. I fell asleep on top of my book, actually, and when I woke up this morning, my cheek was stuck to one of the pages and Hedda was making pancakes. She had sneakily stayed over, which I'm not too happy about, but she is nice to have around, and puts Dad in a *waay* less annoying mood than normal.

I am wearing grey bra number one today. It feels really weird, I'm not used to it yet. Isn't it weird that I'll wear one every day for forever? Unless I have a pyjama day and stay on the sofa being quiet. Mum had pyjama days every now and then when she was sad. Dad never has them at all. Maybe he is not sad ever. Or maybe it's because he is happiest when he is in a suit and giving out to people and being far too important to take time off for anything but death. I'd like to show Mum my new bras and tell her about yesterday. Because it was fun, but it would have been even more fun if she was around as well. I think Mum would have liked Hedda, but it is kind of a mother's job to do what she did yesterday. And Dad's girlfriends are going to be filling in for Mum until I'm old enough to not need jobs like that done any more. Which makes me a bit sad. It just seems so unfair. Maybe I am selfish, like Joel said. But I want my mum. I really want my mum.

GIVE ME YOUR ANSWER DO

I drew a few pictures of Daisy today. She has long brown hair, green eyes and freckledy skin, a bit like me, only I have hazel eyes – greeny-brown ones, like Mum had. Daisy is wearing a blue dress that reaches to the floor, because in those days showing your ankles was the equivalent of flashing your bottom, i.e. not on. I think I'll put that she was the daughter of a shopkeeper, because then she'd have money but wouldn't be too rich. Lots of the rich people back then were from English families because Ireland was still a part of England at that time. I think I'd like to make

Daisy kind of a normal girl, not all up herself and spoiled. I don't think I'm spoiled. I know Dad's really rich, but when I lived with my mum, I think we were kind of poor – I never had as much as everyone else, but I only minded that sometimes. Dad doesn't get me everything I want anyway – he is too busy working and buying expensive suits.

Was Joel right? I've been thinking a lot about what he said. And maybe I'm not as fun as I was before Mum died. But I'm really sad, and I don't think I'm going to stop being sad for ages, maybe never. Maybe that is selfish of me. I know that people like to be around other people who are happy. But I can't help it. It's very hard to change the way you feel, deep down inside.

85

TWO DAYS LATER

Dublin, 1896

Dear Diary,

The doctor says I may only have a few days left. My cough is getting worse and sometimes blood comes out of my mouth and my nose. Breathing is difficult.

Mama and Papa went to see a moving picture show this evening. They said it was a marvel, and that they would take me to see it once I am better. Mama said we could go on the new tram, which is supposed to be very convenient. I wish they would not make plans like this because it is not good for them. They have to realise that. It is not good for me either, because I know that these things will not come to pass, not ever.

Mama saw many fine ladies at the show; she described their outfits to me in detail as she stroked my hair. I am sorry that I will never be one of them; Papa had such high hopes of me making a good marriage and helping our family that way, the only way a girl can help, really. My one wish for myself was that my husband would be a kind man who would refrain from beating me with a thumb stick.

When I was small I always wanted to work in the shop, to help Papa with the ledgers and organising the produce. The boxes that came in, full of exotic things like tea and oranges, were like gifts, and when we had deliveries it was like Christmas morning; lots of things to open and to look at. When I left school, I did get to

work behind the counter now and then, but I always knew that the shop would be my brother's to manage in time, no matter how quick I was at adding prices. I am only a girl, I suppose. I cannot even vote or be allowed to make decisions for myself. And as it stands, I cannot even get out of my bed, lace up my dreaded corset that used to make me faint from lack of breath, or help Mama to set the breakfast table or Papa to take things out of boxes. I would like to have been more useful before I died. Less of a burden.

Of course, I'm not as great a loss as Hugh would be. He hasn't been to see me. He was sickly as a child, and they worry that I might be catching. I would so have liked to have lived to see the turn of the century. 1900 is scarcely four years away - isn't that amazing? I am tired now. So very tired.

Yours,

Daisy.

87

I'm really proud of this. I think it is the most I have ever written for an essay. I printed off some pictures to go with it as well – old black and white ones I found online: the trams and the Abbey theatre and a girl with a serious mouth and smiling eyes. I'm glad it's finished because now I have no more homework to do, and can spend the next two days lazing about without worrying.

Doctors weren't as good back then, so people could die of things we can cure now. Also, they didn't have anti-bacterial hand soap or proper flushy toilets like we do now, so there were loads of germs around and they couldn't get rid of them as easily. Plus they didn't know about them because germs are teeny and you need a microscope to see them. Rats carried disease back then – I suppose some rats still do, but I don't think people kept them as pets and dressed them up in little rat-clothes. Maybe some people. But I suppose it's still more common to have dogs and cats and maybe even hamsters.

NOT TALKING TO PEOPLE

Joel rang last night. I got Dad to say I wasn't home. I do not want to talk to him. I should not have to feel guilty for remembering my mum and being sad. He was completely out of order there and he tried to put it back on me, like I did something to him, which I did not. I've never once been horrible to him, except just after Mum died, when I went quiet for a whole week and didn't speak at all.

After the funeral. I remember the smell of incense being so strong in my nose and in my mouth, and I had written down something to say about Mum because I was told I should say something and I read my little bit. It went along the lines of 'She was a good mum and I will miss her a lot,' because I couldn't talk too much, and after I'd said it I walked down from the altar and instead of sitting back down beside Dad I went outside, and I knew it was wrong to go outside in the middle of Mum's funeral mass, but I couldn't breathe in there and I couldn't be as brave as other people.

And I kept trying to catch my breath and I couldn't see and I felt like I was going to throw up on the steps by the stone basin where people dip their hands in holy water. It was so scary. And someone, maybe Anne, came out after me and held me really close like the way a mother does, like the way my mother won't again, not ever. And I went back in and took communion and kneeled at the right places and let everyone shake my hand and tell me things to make themselves feel better. But it was like being covered with a veil or a lace curtain. I couldn't really see or understand. Not that I was blind or anything. Dazed might be a word I could use. But it wasn't exactly that either. I don't know what it was, but it wasn't very nice, as feelings go.

I didn't talk to anyone for a week after that. I couldn't see the point in speaking. There was nothing I could say to make it better. And after that, when I began to talk, there was still nothing I could say to make it better. I couldn't see the point in being quiet. And I was making people worried and annoyed and like it was all about me, but it wasn't. None of it was. The man who ran over my mother, and conveniently drove off because he was 'in shock', Brian McAllister, still has his house and his kids and his wife and his dog. And they, his children, are allowed to have their mother and their father still.

It hasn't gone to court yet. But he won't be allowed to drive until it does. He'll have to get lifts or cycle, like Mum did. She failed her driving test three times and got it on the fourth. But she preferred to cycle because work was close by and she wanted to keep fit. She liked to cycle and to walk. Even when it was raining. She had a little old car for when we went visiting or on holidays. She'd visit friends from college or school or places she used to work.

Mum had a lot of friends. They were very important because her parents passed away – Granddad when I was three (I don't remember him) and my Nan when I was almost seven (she always had pink sweets with chocolate in the middle in her pocket and she smelled like oranges and dust) and Mum didn't have any brothers and sisters – her parents were old, older than other people's parents were, when they had her. She said that she was spoiled. I don't think she was; she never seemed spoiled to me, although maybe that means that I am spoiled as well. I don't know.

I'm almost looking forward to going back to school. I think I think too much when I'm on holidays because I don't have as many things to do: tidying my room, filling or emptying the dishwasher, looking after my rat, watching TV and reading. Tomorrow I might walk to the pharmacy and get some more hair dye, and maybe I'll ask Ciara to come over in the evening and help me with it.

A SPY IN THE HOUSE

91

Okay, I was really bored, and I did everything I was going to do and I still had hours before Ciara was due to call over. So I started snooping in Dad's room. Well, I started off looking for my hairbrush, and I couldn't find it anywhere (it was on my nightstand) so I kind of had to check Dad's room, and while I was in there I kind of had to rummage around in his drawers, under his mattress and in the boxes at the bottom of his wardrobe. I mean, I'm only human. I didn't find anything too interesting, just boring papers, an old passport (from the oh-my-god-what-have-you-done-to-your-hair years) and some used ticket stubs from plays and hurling matches.

I was all snooped out after my search and I certainly wasn't expecting to find anything when I went to his laptop (his password is Fin2cool007, which says a LOT about him. Like that he would like to be a suave, British secret agent, but in reality is middle-aged and slightly pathetic and not as 2cool as he thinks he is. NOTE TO SELF: on April Fool's Day, change his password to Fin2tool007 and watch him stress). I only wanted to look at videos of kittens sneezing and then falling over to take my mind off how interesting Moustache Hamilton's room had not been.

Then I stumbled across a folder marked 'Primrose' inside another folder marked 'private' (once again, I'm only human). And guess what I found?

It's a letter.

About Mum.

Apparently she kept a diary. Diaries, actually, every year from when she was a teenager. And Dad has decided, in his infinite wisdom, that I shouldn't get them till my sixteenth birthday. He saved a couple of drafts of an email to Uncle Patsy before he sent it, because he saves copies of all his 'correspondence' in case he gets accused of anything or somebody wants to write a biography about the twenty-first century's most boring and pathetic men of business. I didn't think Uncle Patsy and the fluffy one were close at all, but apparently it's easy to keep enormous secrets from me in spite of my suspicious nature and keen eye for snooping.

They're bound to be in the safe, Mum's diaries. But I searched and I searched and I can't find the key. I even tried to open it the way you see on TV, with the hairpin and everything. I mean, they've got to be in there, it's where he keeps all his important stuff. But I did kind of lay waste to Dad's room; his facial hair will be all a-quiver if I don't get it tidy before he comes home. I don't really care about making him angry, but I really, really want to keep him in the dark about this. If he knows I'm searching for the diaries, he is going to go completely crazy and be all clever about hiding them some place I won't be able to look, like in his office, or in his locker at the stupid golf club. I have to be calm and mature about this. I'll tidy his room and tomorrow I'll search the office and every other room he spends time in that has nooks.

This is amazing news, though; I might get to find out all kinds of stuff about Mum, and about Dad too. I hope there aren't any shocking revelations in it. I think I've been bounced about enough for the past while and I don't need any more of

ALL A-QUIVER: Wobbly but a trembly sort of wobble, like the nose of a baby rabbit. Only, in Fin2cool's case, wobbly with rage!

REVELATIONS: Interesting pieces of news or gossip. Things that make you go 'GASP!' and 'ooh!'. There is a book of them in the bible, which is no doubt full of punch-ups and family drama.

93

that. It's weird – before I found out about it, I was just killing time, spying on my father in his own home, but now I know this exists I have to have it, to know what it says about me and about her. I imagine it will be like a bit of her personality, of who she was and who she used to be before I knew her, preserved in notebooks like a fly can be in amber or a fossil in rock. I imagine being able to see and touch it, heavy and real and *there* in a way that memories are not. I don't know how I'm going to be able to be normal around Dad this evening, and Ciara when she comes over, as all I can think about is getting my hands on the diaries.

Okay, I really have to tidy Dad's room now; he'll be home from work really, really soon.

94

DISTRACTIONS

I am back at school, with lovely black hair (although I did make the tops of my ears a blue-y black colour for a day and had to scrub them like mad with a nail brush to avoid looking like a chimney sweep everytime I wore a ponytail). Ciara was very good. She thought of some really sensible things I wouldn't have copped on to, like using old towels and wearing an old T-shirt because I don't want to ruin the newer and more expensive things. Well, not that I care, but it would really tick Dad off and who needs that, when there's covert sneaking and diary-locating to be done? I didn't say a word to her about the diary; it's too private. I probably wouldn't have told Joel yet, even if he wasn't being such a rancid scab of a boy.

I am in another, far superior boy's room at the moment. Ella is too, actually. She is sitting on Felix's bed reading and tapping her fingers in a way that's really annoying me. But it is kind of nice that she wants to hang out, even if hanging out doesn't involve actual talking, just me doing homework and her being dippy. That's mean, but there's no other way to describe it really. She's got this weirdly calm and smiley look on her face and she's just tapping away.

Mary was telling me a bit about what Asperger's is: that's the name of what Ella has. I thought she was autistic, and she is, but if you're only mildly that way it's called Asperger's syndrome. If she was really bad, she wouldn't be able to be in normal school at all. But the way she doesn't really seem to like company all that much and the way she talks and the way she's always drawing animals and talking about animals and the way that, if you're talking to her, she will sometimes just say whatever she wants anyway, as if she didn't hear you or understand what you were saying at all, is a part of it.

She had a rabbit called Mr Rabbit before; she used to always go on about it, but it died a year ago. Mr Rabbit broke Mary's heart. Apparently, he was not only a rabbit but a criminal, biting people who were not Ella and trying to dig holes in sofas and carpets and beds. Eventually he bit a neighbour's child in a fit of pique and from then on he had to be confined to his hutch, and only be taken out on a leash. Mary said 'If I could have got a muzzle as well for the little sod I would have done,' and she showed me a scar on her hand, on the soft skin between her index finger and her thumb, where he had chomped on her as she was feeding him some lettuce.

In his hutch prison, Mr Rabbit got fatter and fatter and more and more malevolent and full of rage. He was more fiercely bad than the rabbit in *The Tale of the Fierce Bad Rabbit*. Ella seemed to like him, though, and she was the only one he would let pet him or pick him up unbitten. I think that's kind of cool. Roderick can be suspicious of new people, but if they're nice to him he's a dreadful flirt, all snuggly and affectionate and licking them on the hand as if he were a dog and not a rat at all. He only rolls over on his back for people he really trusts, though, the chosen few tummy-scratchers: Mum, Joel and me.

Mary is thinking of getting Ella another pet. I recommended a rat, and she looked at me as if I had recommended buying a poisonous snake or giving Ella to a dangerous stranger in a car, offering sweets. She said we might take a trip to the pound tomorrow and see what we could find. I got the distinct impression that whatever we found, it would definitely not be a rat. She is a dreadful pet-bigot, but I like her anyway; she's one of those adults that explains things to me as if I am as intelligent as she is. There's no talking down. I think sometimes she gets a bit sad when she is talking to me, though; she ruffles my hair the odd time in a weird way.

RANCID: Rotten, rotting. Meat that has gone off and begun to smell bad would be rancid. Kind of gross and maggoty. Like Joel.

PIQUE: Anger, spite, annoyance, all round humph!-iness. May involve dramatic head tossing and eye-rolling.

MALEVOLENT: Evil, with intentions of doing bad stuff. The witch in the cartoon of Sleeping Beauty is called Maleficent, which isn't the same word, but it's what I always think of when I think of 'malevolent'. Maleficent was quite malevolent. Which would be very hard to say five times in a row really quickly.

BIGOT: Someone who is predjudiced against people who are different, like people who have different colour skin, or believe different things, or don't live in proper houses. Mary isn't really a bigot in the horrible sense, she just doesn't like rats because she doesn't know any better. Wait until she meets Roderick.

FELIX AND THE CAT

Ella has a new pet: a kitten called Mr Cat. I think Mr Cat might be a girl but I'm not sure. Felix came with us to the pound. It was weird: I was staring at the back of his head in the car, thinking about how much I know about him even though I hadn't seen him before. He's quite good-looking, in a floppy kind of way. He slouches a lot and has quite a low, mumbly way of talking.

He and Ella get on pretty well – he's not one of those older brothers who thinks that younger kids are kind of beneath him. He's not, like, too cool to speak to you or anything. Not that I've said much to him. It's too weird and I get a bit blushy and stupid and amn't able to think of anything sensible to say. Even when he asked me what I thought of some of the animals – like this really excitable puppy who was just so happy to be petted – all I said was, 'He's mostly brown, except his ears.' Or, 'I like his ears.' What, pray tell, is that about? He probably thinks I'm, like, obsessed with ears now. He'll probably think of me as 'ear girl'. And I don't want to be 'ear girl'. I want to be 'cool girl' or 'pretty girl' or 'that girl who is both cool and pretty and who dresses well and for whom I feel an inescapable urge to buy presents'.

He did like my suggestion of Mr Whiskers for the cat's name, though. Ella vetoed it because 'He is a kitten who will grow into a cat and not a whisker, although he does have whiskers.' She was making more sense than I was today. She wouldn't get the puppy because she said he had worms, because he had 'a distended stomach and a hot, dry nose'. Mr Cat, however, got a clean bill of health from her. He was the quietest of the litter that we saw. He tried to hide behind a bin and everything.

Mr Cat is black with white socks. He was found in a box on the side of the road with all his brothers and sisters. He or she, I mean. It's really hard to remember to refer to Mr Cat as a possible she because she is a Mr Maybe-She-is-a-He. It's hard to tell because I haven't had the chance to pet him/her yet, much less get all up in his/her areas.

Ella knows a lot about animals; she asked about specific vaccinations that the kitten might have had and what brand of cat litter they used in the pound, so Mr Cat would be easier to toilet train. She was very particular about the food we bought in the pet shop. It had to have added protein, for some reason. Mr Cat hasn't taken to anyone yet. He is very shy and likes to hide under things. It was a bit of an ordeal getting him out of the car. Me and Ella and Felix were being all gentle and calm-voiced, proffering little pieces of fish and so on. After about twenty minutes of watching us, Mary said, 'Sod this for a game of soldiers,' (what does that mean?) and used the sweeping-brush handle to poke him out from under the seat, scooped him up and lashed him into a cardboard box lined with blankets in their utility room. Ella instructed us to leave him alone, but she has been going in there and making soothing noises all afternoon.

Mr Cat is very quiet, apart from the odd piteous miaow. Felix is in his room. I can hear his music through the ceiling. I am finished my homework, bored, bored bored. Joel texted today.

R U still mad?

I was really tempted to reply

What do u think, assface?

but I refrained, because I have the moral high ground and he is not worth my time.

DISTENDED: A word Ella taught me – it means swollen, bulgy. For example 'After I ate the entire tub of Ben and Jerry's I had a distended stomach.' Mum used to call that a 'food baby' and pat her tum accordingly, with an air of love and pride.

ORDEAL: A difficult experience, for example having your best friend slobber on you in a kissy manner, as though you were a delicious biscuit. Also prison would be an ordeal.

ASS: To put it in a lady-like manner, the part of your body that you sit upon. Obviously. But it can also mean a donkey or a fool - all of which might describe a certain student at St John of God's who shall remain nameless.

THE MORAL HIGH GROUND: Where people who are in the right live. If you have the moral high ground you are right and fabulous and all the Joels who diasagree with you are just wrong.

UGH, YAY AND ???: THREE PIECES OF NEWS FROM OUR CLASS

Karen and Caleb are a couple. Me and Ciara have started calling them 'the Axis of Evil' after the bad guys in World War Two, which we are learning about. Well, watching a DVD about. Karen is totally Germany. They hold hands in the corridors and push the other kids around in various ways: Caleb with his fists, Karen with her words. They must really miss primary school, where everyone was smaller than they were, at least by the end. Now they only have ninety-odd First Years to bully. Which must limit their self-expression a lot. And when they're not hanging around each other, we have to listen to Karen going on about their 'relationship' and how 'into her' he is. Urrgh. They are welcome to each other, even if it does not bode well for bullyable folk around the school. Also Karen has been applying lip balm like nobody's business; her mouth looks like an oil slick, if oil slicks were bubblegum pink and smelled like cherry lollipops. But she needs it because she has a boyfriend now, and they kiss and everything. Get it? *Get it?* Ugh, I can't stand people who are all, 'Look at me, look at *meeeeee*!!!'

Ciara has begun wearing hats to school. She is trying to not eat her own hair any more, because she coughed up a hairball over the weekend, like a cat, and does not care to repeat the experience. She has a different hat for every day of the week. I like her electric blue beret best because it makes her look all cute and French with her wavy dark hair and big brown eyes. Also, when I see her go to chew her hair, I am to tap her hand – or whistle, if I am not sitting beside her. I have been given out to twelve times this week for whistling and will probably get extra homework because of it. It is kind of fun, though, like a secret code that everyone can hear. I have an extremely piercing whistle, like a train or a car alarm. I am not surprised that it puts them off teaching, just gratified and hugely proud. Especially that I annoyed Sr Gloria, because she is a woman of God and should be above all the petty whistlings of us sinners. Only she isn't because she has ears and I have lips. Shudder.

Siobhán's dad lost his job and she is pretty sad about it. I know we don't like her, but that still kind of sucks. She might have to move. Ciara says she's not the worst of the three witches, she just likes being in the group and will follow orders so she can stay a part of it. Not that there are orders, exactly. Basically, she'll agree with Karen on just about anything. BUT there was this awesome moment today where Karen told her to 'Stop going on about it, it's not like he's dead or anything,' and I gave them a daggers look and they went all quiet. Ha. I have the power. The power to remind people about my dead mother and make them feel guilty for saying stupid stuff. It isn't top of the league as far as superpowers go but it is the only one I have and I intend to use it wisely. The whole 'wet the bed' thing isn't going away either: Ella asked me about it the last day. I told her Karen was a liar and a bully. Best to be direct about stuff like that. I hope she never says anything about it in front of Felix. The shame.

SOMETIMES, I LIKE MY DAD

Overheard him on the phone to Hedda. He was talking about the guy who killed Mum, and he was all 'I hope they crucify the *expletive deleted*, Hedda.' It made me smile. Not out of grim satisfaction; I mean, he didn't mean to kill Mum, he's not a murderer, just a stupid, thoughtless man. And I know taking him away from his kids won't bring Mum back. Well, duh. But it's right that he should pay in some way. He stole her life, and the parts of my life she would have been in. I mean, I know it's never going to be easy, losing your mum, but the way in which I lost her was pretty horribly hard, and overhearing Dad get angry about it, even after all these months of not discussing it – well, it made me realise that she was important to him too.

And if his children (I mean, Mr McWhatsit's children, not Dad's, cos that's only me, as far as I know) lose him for a year or five or whatever slap-on-the-wrist punishment they give him, that's not as bad as forever. Forever is very long. I think I should get the option of mowing his wife or one of his kids down in a car while he watches. Not that I'd do it, but so that he would know the fear, the horrible drag-you-deep-downishness of the fear that he rammed home to me the day I realised that everything is breakable.

Also, I think overhearing grown-ups swear in ways that would get them grounded for a good long time if they were my age is pretty funny. Mum rarely swore. She used to work in a nursery school and broke the habit then. Instead of cursing she would go floral, 'oopsy daisy', 'lily-of-the-valley' and 'sun of a flower' being her favourites. I used to get embarrassed when she'd do that in front of my friends, because it was kind of put-on and abnormal and I used to mock her for it before anyone else could.

She was really gentle and floaty in ways like that, like a butterfly. I can't imagine her and Dad ever being a couple. He's all angles and laptops and she was all silk scarves and environmentally-friendly cleaning products. I tried to catch a butterfly by its wings once when I was a toddler. It had landed on the slabs of pavement in our garden and it was blue and white and yellow – all of the colours that mean summertime and happiness. My stubby little fingers broke its wings to powder and I burst into tears because I felt like I had done something terribly wrong. It was the first time I had gotten so close to something so beautiful. And when its wings were gone, it was just another insect. I was more careful the next time and never did a thing like that again.

SIGH

Today was so relaxed. School was fine, we finished that WW2 DVD in double history after break. Dad picked me up and dropped me at Triona's. I had cancelled, so I pretended to go in, waited on the stairs and went to Café Crème again. Smooth.

After that, Dad took me to the cinema. We saw a film about a haunted castle that this family moves into and they have to solve a mystery from two hundred years before to get this ghost to go away. It wasn't scary, though. It was pretty funny and kind of interesting. I wonder if I'd look good in a long white veil.

Dad was asking me questions about Joel and why he hasn't heard much about him in a while. I said that that was my business. He said okay, but Anne had been ringing him to try and find out because she was worried. Ha. So she should be; her precious son is devious and two-faced, and Marcus might go the same way if she's not careful. Joel has been ringing and texting. I think he is sorry, but I do not want to talk to him yet, because if I talk to him I will either rip his head off and feast on his delicious brains or start to cry. Probably the latter.

I am staying at Ciara's house tomorrow night because Hedda and Dad are going to a wedding. I hope this doesn't give him ideas. The last thing I need is a stepmother, even if she's not wicked at all.

Mr Lawless (ha) is the solicitor of Brian McAllister, or as I like to call him, Brian Mc Glug-glug Vroom-vroom. Seven days to go. I don't know if I want to be in the courtroom. I think I am allowed to be. But it will probably just make me feel sick and not do any good. I'd like to have superpowers at times like this, to be able to blast him with laser eyes (the weapony kind, not the ones advertised on telly) or turn invisible and pinch him and pinch him and pinch him. I wonder if he dreams about Mum, like I do, and then wakes up in the middle of the night and can't get back to sleep and has to lie there waiting for the morning. Sometimes I get up in the middle of the night, when I can't sleep, and get a drink of water.

Recently, I've been very quietly looking around for Mum's diaries as well. I've done all the rooms except Dad's office and the attic above the garage. Both of those are going to be tricky, but fingers crossed I'll finally get somewhere. I wish I was more agile, like Roderick. He is only small but can find ways to scale bookshelves, television stands and wardrobes. Although he is currently cleaning his ear with his toes and then eating what he has scraped out. So he has his flaws too. It must be great to be a rat and not have to be nice or hygenic or anything but greedy for food, cuddles and adventures, in that order. Those are some nice priorities. I miss hugs, the soft, warm, comforting, Mummy kind of hugs, as opposed to the odd, suited, aftershavey squeeze I get from the moustached one. The old hugs had a way of making me feel better, like I was very safe and very loved. I don't feel safe any more. I feel threatened, like something could go wrong at any moment. Shudder. Time for a change of subject. I might run down and see what's on TV.

DISPATCHES FROM A STRANGE LOCATION

I am in Ciara's room – it's, like, twice or three times the size of my room and covered with posters and pictures cut out of magazines and so on. So much handsome blandness on the walls, lots of sparkling eyes and teeth topped by floppy, choppy, utterly spotless hair. It's very hard for me not to make smart comments but I will be strong and swallow them because I know she feels the same way about Roderick and all the cluttery boxes of CDs, books and DVDs etc in my room. She is all neat, and my room is a tip, albeit a ladylike, comforting, reasonably floral one. It looks like I'm just after moving in or have recently returned from a holiday. Constance, the cleaning lady Dad hires to nip in and out for a couple of hours, three mornings a week (I have never seen her, but things get washed and folded and dusted, and it's certainly not me or Dad doing it), doesn't go near my room, partly because of Roderick and partly because 'it will do me no good at all to be waited on hand and foot'. What would I learn? Apart from the joy of living in cleanly bliss as opposed to messy okay-ishness.

Ciara's room is scarily tidy. She has separate (labelled) drawers for trousers, skirts, jumpers and dresses. I keep mine on the floor for easy access – well, the ones I've worn recently, anyway. On the plus side, she also has an amazing box of hats and a digital camera, so we have spent the past hour and a half putting on hats and doing our hair to suit the hats and taking pictures of ourselves, deleting those where we look less than spectacular. Lots of pouting and flattering smiles, where you only show some teeth – my real smile is a manic semi-circle of lips and teeth, like my face has been cracked in half by a grin. More of a 'beam' than a smile, really.

Ciara has a lovely smile, but she probably practised it. She is awfully together in most ways. She never bites her nails; she files them into perfect pink and white oval shapes, like a proper lady – a film star, or the rich wife of a rich man. Or Dad's ex, Cynthia, come to think of it. She had lovely nails – mainly because she'd never done a day's work in her life, according to Mum, whose nail varnish was always a bit chipped. I've never done a day's work in my life either, so I probably shouldn't be all judgey, but I totally will have worked by the time I'm in my twenties. I have hardly any nails at all – they're bitten to the quick – but at least I don't eat my own hair, so ha.

There was a lot of whistling this evening. Her whole family is in on it, helping her to not chew her hair any more, so any time she even looks like she's thinking about it, or puts up her hand to scratch her head or anything, everyone lets out a piercing whistle to gently (loudly and irritatingly) remind her not to have a bit of an aul munch on her delicious curls. I think if I were Ciara I would have killed them all by now and eaten myself bald just to spite them. But she's more well-adjusted than me that way, I suppose.

Her family are pretty annoying, all picture-perfect and well-groomed. Her parents play golf together and still hold hands and kiss when they think nobody's looking. Shudder. Also, pressure much? If Ciara wants to meet the man of her dreams at the same age as her mum met her dad, she has less than two years left. Arrgh. Her dad wears colouredy argyle jumper vests and try-hard 'hip' glasses to counteract his obvious comb-over. Fintan would probably happily go for pints with him, actually.

How boring would that be, though, to meet someone before you got the chance to have any fun? I want at least thirty boyfriends before I settle down, and I'm breaking up with all of them first. You need some good stories to shock people with when you're a pensioner. Otherwise, all you'd have would be a bus pass, a measly little pension and a rake of dead friends. Also I want one of those enormous shopping baskets on wheels that little old ladies have – practical and stylish! I once tried to convince Mum to buy me one by way of a schoolbag, but she was having none of it, which was good, because it would have probably been

111

equivalent to prancing into school with 'Bully me, please, as it would most likely benefit me greatly' tattooed across my forehead.

IN-MUM-NIA

I couldn't sleep last night. I kept thinking about the trial date, and Mum and Joel and Dad and every embarrassing or stupid or bad thing I've ever done, like that time I was four and weed in a shop because Mum wouldn't buy me a bright pink vinyl handbag with kittens on it, or the time I was ten and I accidentally stepped on a homeless man in the park and ran away afterwards because I was scared, and never said sorry. I have such a pain in my tummy; I feel like something terrible is going to happen.

I finally told Ciara about my search for Mum's diary and we tried to think of a way for me to get a look around Dad's office. And also other places it could be hidden. She suggested that it might be in a safety deposit box but surely those are only in American action movies about people with secret agendas and multiple identities and not about middle-aged men who should know better than to 'jazz up' their suits with funky ties with patterns like popcorn buckets and other things that should not be on ties ever, ever, ever.

Ciara told me a secret about herself, too. She has been clandestinely texting the lovely Syzmon. This is weird because she doesn't really talk to him or look at him any more when we are in school. But they do live kind of close to each other, and apparently they sometimes walk to the bus-stop together, and once, they missed the bus and just walked all the way home. She says it's the weirdest thing but also the nicest, and she doesn't want to ruin it by having everyone making comments and so on.

Karen and them still have a HUGE influence on her; she worries about what they'll think or what nasty things they might say, etc. Which is dumber than a headless Barbie doll because Karen is kissing

COUNTERACT: To act like a counter, i.e. to lie around in kitchens with saucepans and kitchen roll balanced on you. Not really, though. It means to balance out, or cancel out. Like Ciara's Dad growing his hair long on one side, and flopping it over the top of his head in a brave, yet foolish attempt to counteract his inherent bald-as-an-egg-iness.

PENSIONER: Someone old, over sixty-five, who gets a pension, which is money you get when you're not able to work any more or can't be bothered to.

EQUIVALENT TO: Equal to, the same as.

Caleb and so is hardly a bastion of taste and coolness. So there! Hmm...

I'm glad she told me, and he's a sweet boy, but *ick ick ick* – not that they're friends, because that's lovely and she deserves lots of friends after her bad time at the beginning of the year, but I think she LIKE likes him, and it makes me wonder if this is the beginning of it, where hormones kick in and we all start wanting to do unspeakable things to each other behind cinemas and on the dance floors of alcohol-free discos. I don't want to do unspeakable things to anyone in particular just now, although I would quite like to smell Felix's neck at close range (he has a charming nape).

SECRETS THAT I COULD FIND OUT FROM MUM'S OLD DIARIES

 My real daddy is a king: unlikely, as Papa Bear probably made her take a paternity test before he parted with a red cent of his hard-earned wealth. He is a canny businessman and not a very trusting individual. For example, he has recently taken to locking his bedroom door when he leaves the house in the morning (can't think why), quite forgetting that there is a spare key for it in the enormous box labelled *Box o' Keys* which he keeps in the kitchen. But if my real daddy were a king, I would still be

living with a rich, irritating virtual stranger,
only this time I'd have tiaras and ballgowns
and other awesomely fancy things – carriages
and dancing slippers, which are like real
slippers, only not fluffy and shaped like teddy
bears (mine) or pints of guinness (Dad's,
shudder), so basically thin dancing shoes you
can't go outside in unless you want to mess
them up completely and make your father, the
king, suspicious enough to send a creepy old
soldier after you and your eleven sisters. I get
my king-formation from fairy tales as opposed
to tacky magazines, because I would like to be
the kind of princess who does not get
photographed in a bikini to promote her latest
project. Actually, I would not like to be
photographed in a bikini at all – I'm all oddly-
shaped at the moment, with my hips (amongst
other things) getting bigger and slightly hairier
(*eww*), so any picture of me would be easy to
caption in a mean and tacky way. Not that I'm
a total freak or anything. Some days I look
okay. Maybe not Ciara-good (she looks like a
pixie in a film, all small and pointy and
delicate). But me-good, which is kind of a
happy okay, like the way an enthusiastic
drama teacher would start a warm-up game,
like, 'Oh-kayyy!'.

115

That she knew her killer. Brian McAlli-start-drinking-at-two-o-clock-in-the-day-and-then-drive-home. There could be evidence that it was malicious. Okay, that's not very likely, but it would make more sense than what actually did happen which is just a random, stupid accident. Also, if I could prove it was murder as opposed to drunk driving, then he'd get longer in prison. Which wouldn't bring my mum back, but would keep him off the road and reflecting on the stupid horrible thing he did to my family of two (okay, two and a half – I suppose I have to count Dad a bit).

What really happened with her and Dad: this is a big one, because all they ever said was that they were together for a while but it didn't work out, and that they both love me very much. But there was sometimes a kind of angry vibe between them and maybe it had to do with me. I mean, I can be quite the little scamp with my rat-sidekick and my plans for world domination (watch this space), but maybe it had to do with their past. I'd quite like to know how two such different people ended up having a baby together, aside from the obvious and disgusting how. The feelingsy side of it all: I'd like to understand that; it might help me be happier about where I come from. My people.

What Mum's family were really like. There's no one left to tell me – she was an only child and her parents died when I was young. I didn't really know them as people, as opposed to friendly hug-and-sweet-providing beings with silvery hair and thick Kerry accents. Mum lost her accent because she went to the Protestant school. I don't know how being around Protestants makes you speak more clearly, but that's what she said. She never really took me to church all that much, but when we did go it was to Catholic mass so the Protestants obviously didn't convert her to their ways. Not that I know what their ways are – I imagine it's pretty much the same. Only with posher accents, maybe. At least in Kerry.

117

 That she never liked Joel to begin with and knew that we would fall out one day, what with his being the dark prince of the toad-folk and all. I do kind of miss him, though. I haven't put a moustache on a baby in a very long time – almost a month! This really will not stand. Mum liked Joel, I think (although I could be wrong, because I don't have access to her diary yet). She used to always say it was important to have friends of the opposite sex (oh, my!) because that's the way the world is, and so on and so forth. She was a great fan of the saying 'It takes all sorts to make a world,' to which I would usually say, 'Well, duh!'

That she faked her own death to escape from a crew of assassins and wants me to meet her in the Cayman Islands, where I will complete my schooling in a tropical paradise and have a pet macaw of my very own. Not likely, but it's nice to think about. Also a bit sad-making, though. You know the way stupid hope is the saddest thing to see in films, like the man who comes home with a smile and an engagement ring while his girlfriend is kissing the postman passionately (although not Postman Pat. He was far too dignified and moral for any sort of deceptive carry-on). Or the girl who comes home with an A on a test for her mother to stick on the fridge, hoping for celebratory ice-cream, only to run into a neighbour with a sad face and some terrible news. That kind of thing really upsets me. It just doesn't seem fair.

118

PATERNITY TEST: A test you can get a doctor to do to tell if you are the daddy of a baby or child or even a grown-up. Ladies do not have to do these tests because they usually remember having a baby.

I GET A ROW (ROW, GET A ROW, I GET A ROW)

It's rainy and horrible and I just had a blazing row with Fintan. The Triona thing finally came back to bite me in the bottom. She called him today to check that I was going to 'continue my treatment'. And Dad kept yodelling on about how important it was for me to see Triona and process my grief and talk out my feelings and other stupid things that I don't actually do in those stupid, awkward, expensive sessions in that ugly office. I mean, just being in there makes me depressed; it's so thought-out, trying to be jolly with its photos and false flowers. (I don't see the point of false flowers. They're never as nice as the real thing, which she is too cheap to buy, even with all the cheques and gold she gets for listening to people spew out their problems while pursing up her mouth in a way that says 'Smack me, smack me right in the face, it's just what I deserve for being so obnoxious.') But enough moaning about what a bland excuse for a person she is and back to my current enemy. He was all nasty and self-righteous.

'I don't care how you feel about it; Triona is the best doctor in the business and you are going to keep seeing her until I am satisfied that you are okay.'

Wrong, wrong, wrong wrong, wrong! Ugh, just because he got her card off some guy at work whose daughter stopped eating for, like, a year doesn't mean she's not an unlikeable snore of a woman, as boring as a cardboard box full of plank after plank after plank.

Dad wouldn't even let me finish saying that, though. He was off on another rant.

'You mope around the house all day being surly and antisocial.'

Ugh! Wrong again, Fintan McFoolish. You have to make a choice to be antisocial and Joel not being around kind of limits what I get up to in the evenings and on weekends, because there is really only so much Ciara I can take, and I get it all during the week, which is when I also get my dose of Ella-time. And why shouldn't I hang out in my own house? Well, his house, but it is supposed to be mine as well. Urrgh.

And what's with Triona being such a tattler? I mean, GOD! Business must be pretty slow if she can't afford to lose even one resentful, surly bag of woe from her stack of damaged goods. Ha! Maybe everyone else hates her as much as I do and are all leaving her to stew in her rancid juices, humming at thin air. That's what she does, she goes 'Hummmmm ... And how does that make you feel? And why do you think you think that?' and a plethora of other questions that are so confusing that all I can do is blink back my frustration and the all-encompassing urge to rock back and forth chanting endlessly for her to go away, go away, go away ... until she actually does. Which she never will because Dad gives her one hundred euro an hour and she's not a complete moron – cha-ching!

So, I am now going to be walked right up to her office every Friday.

'I will literally drag you in if I have to, Rosie.' (I hope he does, then I'll totally ring Childline; that'd show him.)

And afterwards, I will be picked up right outside her door. Because I cannot be trusted. He was all, 'What have you been doing, Primrose?' (Using his negotiating thing where you say the person's name to put them at ease, but it really is just creepy and weird when you try to use it on your daughter who has been going through your personal papers every other day, looking for clues that could lead to diary-location.)

I told him I had been working part-time as a drug mule, but I hoped to work my way up to dealing eventually.

And he was all grrr-faced and 'Don't be so glib.'

And I told him not to be so glob, which isn't even a word but it was the best I could do at the time, given how angry he was making me.

And then he said, 'What would Bláthnaid say if she were alive today?'

And I said that she would probably say, 'Why are you sending my daughter to a grief counsellor seeing as I'm alive, you moron?'

He did not like that at all and said that she would be disappointed in me, and so I retorted with a scathing and insightful, 'Well, you're mean, mean, mean, mean, mean and it's not fair and blllleeeeerghh hhhaghduhguhwahhhhh.'

Can't believe I cried in front of 'Tache-face. He *is* mean, mean, mean, mean, mean.

Blllleeeeergh-hhhha-ghduhguhwahhhhh.

So, once I was crying he gave me a big hug and told me everything would be alright and I didn't have to go back to Triona if the idea of it upset me that much and then we ate some Werther's Original and went fishing on a big sparkly lake, and then a flying pig swooped down and bit a chunk right out of his bottom and, oh, how we laughed.

Right.

What really happened was he got all white and confused-looking and I stormed off to my room to have a good cry and to tell Roderick how useless and old and boring Dad was, and was it my imagination or was his hairline receding? This was all in a very loud voice, behind a very locked door.

It's quieter now, and I'm cuddled in bed – it's really cold, wintry weather. This Christmas is going to be the most depressing thing ever. Ugh. No friends, no Mum and I have to spend it with that moustachioed freak. Hedda might get me something good, though. She's the type who would. She was the one who convinced Dad it would be a good idea for Patsy, Éanna and Phineas to come visit next weekend so I could meet them before I go stay in their house for a week. Ugh! If Dad and I are still raging at each other, this weekend is going to be awkward.

I am kind of looking forward to seeing Phineas, though. Because babies are cute and innocent and rarely tick anyone off with offensive and hurtful behaviour. Also, they can poo in public, grinning away to themselves all the while and no one thinks anything of it, which must be pretty cheering. And I love their fat little arms and legs, all rolly and splodgy and smelling of baby. Baby smell is the best thing. Although Felix has this new deodorant thing that smells pretty fine also, not overpowering and cough-making like some other boys I could care to mention. Joel once cultivated a *grá* for such a powerful scent, and Mum and I used to joke that his manly musk resulted in lots of coughing and possible death by asphyxiation. Anyway, in sum, Felix smells nice, Dad is mean, Triona is going to see me soon and I am not happy in the least about it and will probably stay up reading and worrying

123

and scheming my way out of the Friday session. Maybe if I come down with something contagious, like flu or plague?

PLETHORA: Loads, a lot, a big amount. As in 'Fintan was not blessed with a plethora of sense and good looks.'

GLIB: Insincere, something Fintan accuses me of being because he is a fool. I am never glib. He is the one who is glib, because he is a businessman and lives in the world of the hard sell and the tough break and the meaningless soundbite. He often tells me business is a lot like something that business is not a lot like at all (a woman / a fine meal / a puppy dog). That is glib. He is the one who should not be so glib. He is also the one who should not be so stupid and expensively dressed. So there.

ASPHYXIATION: Chokeage, suffocation, not being able to breathe. This can sometimes be caused by the perviest types of aftershave.

TRIAL AND ERROR

Ugh! Off school today because it is the day of the trial. Realised this morning that I have absolutely no idea what people wear to watch trials. Suits for lawyers and journalists and older people, but I am thirteen and do not have a wardrobe full of well-cut suits in a rake of dull colours. Mostly, I'm glad of that fact, but today? Probably would have been handy. Dad wore a suit. His lawyer wore a suit. I wore a black skirt, a white T-shirt with grey and black knives and forks on it and Mum's baggy cardigan (the one I sleep with – it's a bit eewy but I thought she should be represented in my outfit). Dad raised an eyebrow but decided not to comment, which was a good thing for his health and not-getting-yelled-at-ness. Also, I wore dangly earrings shaped like bicycles, as a kind of dig at the accused. (I haven't worn those earrings since the day of the accident, actually. They used to be one of my favourite pairs, but they aren't any more for obvious reasons.)

Anyway, in the morning, me and Dad went for breakfast in a café that was chock-full of lawyers and lawyerly-looking people, and then to the courthouse where we sat on uncomfortable seats and fidgeted. I was feeling a bit worried, actually. Some of Mum's friends were there, Dave and Méabh and Sorrel. They came over and gave me big hugs right away. They weren't worried about looking like they

125

belonged, but then I suppose it's not something they worry about anyway: Sorrel dresses like a medieval fairy with a penchant for flounce and Dave always wears the same jacket and jeans. Méabh was in her uniform from the museum. She'd obviously taken time off to attend; she's such a sweetheart. She always was, really – making cups of tea and sandwiches for people when they were sad, and always saying things that made you feel better.

I miss Mum's friends. Dad doesn't really have any. Well, just work friends and golf friends – he's not a total loser. But no one that I know, no one who comes around for tea and ruffles my hair and tells me stories, or gives me a rat (thanks, Dave). Hedda, I suppose. But that's different, because they're together. He doesn't really have a close platonic friend, someone he spends time with without schmoozing. As far as I know anyway. That's kind of sad. I'd like to have friends when I'm older, a big circle of warmth to protect me from the bad things that can happen to good people in the world. I don't know if I'll be like Mum that way, when I grow up. I hope I will.

Anyway, back to the courtroom. The lawyers were there. It's not us suing him, it's the State, because it's a criminal thing – I mean, he *killed* a woman, even if he didn't mean to.

It took a while to get going, all statements and going over facts and blah, and his barrister was all going on about how full of remorse the guy was and how he was a 'family man' and the wage-earner in his household. Well, so was Mum. Only a woman, with a smaller family. And responsible wage-earning types of people shouldn't drink a lot and drive over people's mothers, I mean, OF COURSE he's feeling remorseful, anyone would – that's hardly a good thing – it's just a bloody given. There's no need to be all 'Oh, he's feeling rather guilty, so that's punishment enough' about it. Ugh. Needless to say, Judgey-wudgey lapped it up. (I call him that because he was all gravitas and silver hair – I reckon he needs to be taken down a peg or two. At least within my head, and later, to Dad in the car when we were ranting like madmen. Well, madman and dependant anyway.) I reckon they golf together or something, him and the lawyer. They were very cordial, and I saw them talking afterwards with obnoxiously well-fed smiley faces on. Grr. Grr to the power of ARRGGH.

So, after all that, he got four years, which is huge – I mean, it's almost a third of the time I've been alive, and so on. But it's also the minimum sentence for the crime he committed, which kind of sucks. I'm not sure how to feel about it to be honest. I mean, whatever he gets, it isn't going to bring her back and it must be pretty awful for his family – although not as awful as if he were dead, which is what my mother is as a result of him. See my dilemma? I have all these slightly compassionate thoughts, but then I remember Mum's mangled, broken body, and how she used to love cycling around the place. I mean, she always wore a helmet and those ridiculous bright yellow reflective vests that council workers have – that's how careful she was.

And she wanted to live. Well, not that she ever really said, 'I want to live' to me, but, I mean, she was doing a pretty good job of being alive, and nobody says that, really, unless they're in danger of dying and they know it. But we're all in danger of dying pretty much all the time, which is what Mum's death taught me. When I think like that, I get all sick in my tummy, and it's sadness but also anger, because if it was anyone's fault it was his – and at least that's acknowledged, even if it's the bare minimum sentence he gets.

Dad's pretty ticked off, though. He was all sweary and teary and huggy and then sweary again when we got home after the 'travesty of justice', which is what he calls the trial. He went on and on about what a slap in the face it was to the memory of a good woman and how he hopes Brian McNasty-pants gets a cell-mate who enjoys practising the noble art of prison brutality. And then he was all talking about Mum and how she was when he met her, 'the most beautiful creature, so naturally lovely in every way', and how sorry he was that he never got to apologise to her for 'the way I handled things'. (Side note: I really, really want to read her diaries even more now.)

And he told stories about when I was small, and how, even though they weren't getting on, they'd take me places together because they thought it was good for me, and how I kind of made them be friends again because they had this bond (me). Lots and lots of sentimental nonsense along those lines, and I was really surprised by it, because he'd never really talked to me this way before, not even just after she died. And it was kind of a relief to know he cared so much, that he could get so het up about it. We stayed up until very late swapping stories, and he said I could have the day off school tomorrow because it's three o' clock in the morning now and I'm probably going to be up thinking for a while yet.

Oh, Joel texted as well, around eight o'clock.

```
Mum  told  me  wat  happened  today:
really  sorry  abt  that  and  abt  us
not   speaking,   but   if   u   need
anyting  call  me    no  matter  what
I'm  here  4  u.
```

I thought that was nice, and decided to reply even though at this stage I had a crying daddy on my hands. I said,

```
thanks  for  that,  it's  ok.  might
chat  soon.
```

And we might. I'd like to be his friend again, but first he has to do a big apology in person, just so I can feel better about what happened, not so much for the kissy buisness, but for the things he said. I suppose I said some nasty stuff as well. But he totally has to say sorry first. So there.

What a day! I wonder what we'll do tomorrow. Dad says he 'has plans', but he won't tell me what they are. Humph! Yet also oooh?

PENCHANT: a grá, a tendancy towards, a strong liking of. I have a penchant for being awesome. If other people can't accept that, then they are haters and I want nothing more to do with them.

PRIMMY

... is what Dad has started calling me now: Primmy or Prim, which is weird, as it used to be Rosie before. I kind of like it, though. It reminds me of Mum. Which maybe is his devilish plan. Today was quite something, and now I am full of spaghetti from Ciao Bella down the road. It was something else altogether, and there were two kinds of cheese to sprinkle on it: mozzarella and cheddar. Yum! Anyway, greediness aside, today was interesting on many levels. I don't know how I'll go back to school tomorrow. So much has happened; I feel older or like I've been away for a much longer time.

Also, Triona tomorrow afternoon. Bah. And she's going to be all questions and making me talk about the verdict and so on, like a leech in a suit, sucking responses out of me when I don't want to give them. I sometimes feel like I'm her own little soap opera. Every week she gets an update of some way in which I've messed up. I wonder if you have to like hearing about other people's misery to do her job, or is her attitude just an unexpected perk?

This morning I slept in until noon or so, which was lovely, and then Dad took me out for breakfast, to a place he used to go with Mum when they were together. It has changed names now, and apparently the food is more expensive and not as nice, but it was still a lovely thought. Then we fed the birds in the park and rambled around book and music shops together. He bought me a few CDs I wanted and some he 'thought I should have' for my musical education. Poncey much? But it was nice. Also, I got a few new books, which is cool, because I've been reading one of Mum's trashy romance novels, and it is filthy and quite unsuitable for a young impressionable girl like me who might take it too much to heart and run off with a sexy Viking as soon as she turns sixteen. Can't be doing with that sort of thing at all. I am kind of enjoying it, though, in between moments of worrying about my mother's tastes. It's quite sad that she never met a Viking to call her own. Well, I suppose Dave was kind of Vikingy with his untamed hair, but it's not really the same thing if they don't have a longboat and lots of chalices (and other bling ripped off from monasteries) with which to impress a girl.

After the shopping we went to Dad's office and he had his assistant make me tea, and then he literally pushed aside one of the paintings in his office and there was a wall safe behind it and he punched in a combination (there is at least one 6 in it, but couldn't tell more) and took out a notebook with a bookmark in it.

Mum's diary! I thought immediately.

He was all, 'Prim, were you aware your mother kept a diary?'

And I acted all surprised, like, 'Ooh, really, is that it?' while greedily reaching my hand out like the smiley fellow in *The Lord of the Rings*, all 'MINE, MINE at last, muhahhahahahahahahahahaha.'

But he wouldn't give it to me right away. He was all, 'First, there are some things I want to say. I thought about giving these to you just after your mother's death, but you were going through a lot, and after reading them, to be honest, I didn't think you were emotionally mature enough – I still don't.'

That is the point where I was all, 'Um ... what?!!'

'And the decision I reached, after a lot of soul-searching, is that the diaries would be given to you on your sixteenth birthday, but until then I'm keeping them here.'

'So why tell me about them?'

'Well, there is one bit I would like to give to you to read today, and I've made a copy of the entry for you to take home and keep.'

Mighty big of you, Fintan.

He turned the pages until he had reached one he had bookmarked and it was my birthday, my real actual *birth* day – the day I was born. It was about how beautiful I was and how small and wrinkled and how surprised she was by how much she loved me already and how protective she felt, even though the birth had been horrible (small mother, big baby, eighteen hours of *ow*). And she said that even though things might not work out with Fintan (they didn't) and even though this was probably the worst timing ever, she was so proud of her little flower, her Primrose, the best thing she'd ever done. And when I was finished reading, Dad looked at me and I looked back at him and he said, 'You know, she felt that way up until the day she died. She was so proud of you, lovey. But there's personal stuff in there too, things she wouldn't have felt comfortable with you knowing, not just about me, about her friends and life in general. But there isn't one moment in all her diaries where she doesn't feel the strong love that she felt for you the day you were born.'

There were tears in his eyes, because he is an emotional flower and because I was crying a bit too. It was kind of a lovely thing to have, the record of the way she felt when I was too young to remember her.

Also, thank God I didn't stay all pink and wrinkled, gross!! And we dried our tears and then he had his secretary, Kath, bring us tea and scones with jam and cream. It must be nice to have that kind of power, to be all, 'Bring me scones!' and scones arrive ten minutes later. He did say please and thank you, though, as Kath tends to get a bit short when he gets all grumpy and snappish, and he does not want to displease her as she is the most efficient woman in the world and the only one who knows how to wallop the photocopier just right in order to get it working again.

Anyway, after that we drove again and he wouldn't tell me where we were going, but it ended up being to Joel's house and he was all, 'Sorry about this, but I have to drop something off to Anne,' My eye.

I said that I would stay in the car, but he was in there for five minutes when Joel came out and was all, 'You want to go for a walk?' and we did and he apologised for his dreadful deeds and said that it was all his fault for not being honest with me about problems he was having at school. I told him he didn't have to tell me everything unless it would make him feel better, but that he better tell me if he was planning on kissing me again so I could help out and slip him a bit of tongue to make for a more realistic effect! (Obviously I was only joking about that bit, because eww! Not to the kissing, but to the kissing of the Joel.) Anyway, he asked if I wanted to watch a film or something, and I said okay. When we walked back to the house, Dad was there drinking coffee with Anne and chuckling in that weird ingratiating way he does with clients or people he wants to impress. He is getting a bit better, but he is still a freak on many levels.

Obviously it was okay that I stuck around with Joel for the evening, and Dad said he would pick me up at seven so I could get ready for school tomorrow, blerg! Me and Joel watched *Pretty in Pink*, which I love and is one of Mum's favourite films. Joel does not love *Pretty in Pink*, but he was trying to make all nicey nice and I am not such a saint that I would not take advantage of that in order to watch girly stuff and talk along with the characters and sing along with the soundtrack, which I know full well annoys the pants off him (not literally, thank God, or we would argue a lot more than we do).

Anyway, while Molly Ringwald was taking two lovely dresses and sewing them into one hideous crime against debs dresses everywhere, Joel told me why he had kissed me that time. Turns out St John of God's doubles as St John of Sporty, Creepy Assfaces. The boys in his year – well, not all of them, but Liam was one – started calling him a fag because of his awesome dress sense, distaste for sport and occasional mincing. (Okay, I totally made that last one up.) It kind of got out of hand, to the point where they were calling him that instead of his given name and they were doing other yeuchy things too, like hiding his books and replacing them with girly paraphernalia like tights and hair slides and pretty pink socks. He wouldn't have minded that so much, only their taste was atrocious, so he couldn't even pass them on to me.

Unsurprisingly, this was all getting to him quite a bit. I mean, it was bullying-type behaviour, although when I said this he wasn't too gone on calling it that, being all excuse-making, and more, 'Oh, no, that's just the way the lads are,' etc.

So, rather than just chalk it up to them being idiots, he cleverly decided that a false girlfriend would convince them of his heteronormative ways and general manly demeanour. P'shaw, I say! And we would both have been all, 'Sod them' if we were still at the same school, but when you don't have a best friend around to convince you of your awesomeness and general kick-assitude, it can happen, on occasion, that your self-esteem slips a little. And had he explained that to me at the time, I would totally have posed as his girlfriend, or whatever, until either of us met someone we actually wanted to kiss. I mean, what are friends for if not for lies and subterfuge and stopping you getting bullied? But there was no call to get so sneaky and defensive about it, so I'm

HETERONORMATIVE: Boys liking girls and girls liking boys. Predictable romanticky carry-on, like you see in storybooks and Disney films. Some people think this is the best way to be, even if it doesn't make you happy. These people (see bigot) usually talk loudly on their mobiles in restaurants and throw their rubbish in other people's fields. They also may or may not buy puppies, husbands, wives and children and forget to feed, walk and love them. Gah.

MANLY DEMEANOUR: Appearance and general carry-on that reeks of manly. Lumberjacks, outlaws and Clint Eastwood as a cowboy all have manly demeanour without trying. Pirates can have it if they're not over-filthy or wearing too much stolen jewellery. Dad occasionally has this when he does things that are manly, like fixin' drains and hammerin' nails. (Dropping your g's and doing a growly voice can add to your manly demeanour.) Though Mum could do stuff like that without having a manly demeanour or complaining like a whiny girl-child when she got an oil spot on her jacket. Dad is not half the woman she is.

glad he apologised and recognised his own ass-hattery before we drifted apart any more. Also, he told Liam we broke up, so it's not like he's only making up with me to continue his devilish scheme. Because that would suck. Ugh. I hope this whole bullying business isn't a normal secondary school thing that will eventually happen to almost everyone. Because I am not cool with that.

SUBTERFUGE: Must be said with an exclamation point after it, like this: 'Subterfuge!' Plots, schemes and secret plans that are used to achieve your goals. Subterfuge doesn't always have to be a bad thing. Sometimes it is the best way to get what you want. Especially if what you want is sweet, sweet revenge.

Anyway, we had chips and sausages for dinner and chatted about all the news we'd missed out on by not talking to each other, and towards the end of the evening, I also apologised for the mean things I had said. Because even though he was the one who was totally in the wrong, I didn't want him to think that I meant all those things or anything. So that's sorted. Ciara will be happy; she sets great store by having friends who are boys as 'how else will we end up with boyfriends?' She is a single-minded lady and could probably be President one day if she set her mind to it and didn't begin painting all national monuments her favourite shade of pink – cerise – until she was safely in office.

READY FOR THE WEEKEND

... any time now, although it would rule if I could skip Friday afternoon, when I have to see Triona after my long and ultra-voluntary absence. School was yeuchy today: we had a geography test and I didn't know any of the answers because I hadn't been in. Well, I knew a few that were just common sense, but I don't like horrible surprises like that. Also, Ms Smith was all short with me today for not having my English homework done, which is just unfair, because Dad gave me a note and I had a bloody good reason for being absent from school. And I had to tell Ciara about making up with Joel and stuff, and so I kind of had to spend most of the morning whispering and passing notes instead of listening to stuff and writing stuff down.

Karen and Caleb have been moved to different desks because there was a lot of under-desk hand-holding and leg-stroking going on and nobody needs to see that. Shudder. Of course, they are all *Romeo and Juliet*-ing away, giving each other meaningful glances across the room and so on. Oh, how cruel life is to young, bad-minded bullies in love! So cruel!

Ha. Actually, Karen was throwing Caleb *waay* more looks than he was her, because he spent a lot of time and energy carving obscenities into his desk with a compass and then getting a quiet, scary-voiced talk from Ms Smith and a little trip to the principal's office. Which kind of counteracts the whole scary-voice talk, because Ms Cleary is quite kind and jolly compared to angry Lucrezia, and she has a soft spot for poor, misunderstood, horribly destructive Caleb, which makes one of us.

Also, Lucrezia totally has a tattoo. I saw the top of it today. She had a top that was lowish at the back. I didn't like to ask her about it, but it was all gold and brown and teal and feathery, so it's probably something awesome. I'd like to know more about Ms Smith's life outside of school. I bet it's all dramatic and artsy.

Syzmon and Ciara went off for a bit of a talk at break, so I hung around with Ella, talking about Mr Cat and how he likes his tummy scratched a certain way and has developed an irrational hatred of Mary's favourite rug, the blue and red one in the sitting room. Well, hatred of, or love of clawing at. One or the other. Also, he will only drink whole milk and eat things that have fish in them, unless something is left on a plate on the worktop, in which case he will try anything. Mr Cat is easily seduced by the forbidden, the wee scamp. Also, Felix is in a band now, which makes him even more attractive and stalkable. They are called the Deep Tinkers and play music that Ella describes as 'loud' and 'annoying to cats'.

Mr Cat did a wee in Felix's room the last day, and is now being treated like a furry criminal by Mary and Felix. Eep. It's all cleaned up anyway, because I certainly couldn't smell anything when I was doing my homework there, although Ella's house was a wee bit uncomfortable and embarrassing today for other reasons, namely that Mary walked in on me taking a deep and longing sniff of one of Felix's T-shirts. I was all flustered and said, 'I just thought I smelled something funny and I was trying to find out what it was.' She thought I meant the cat pee, and took the T-shirt away to be washed, but what I was really smelling was pure, unadulterated foxy-boy-in-band-smell. Also, I think he might have started smoking, because there is a packet of cigarettes in his sock drawer and his T-shirt smelled of them a bit as well. I normally think yeuch yeuch yeuch when I smell fag smoke, but in his case I might be willing to make a handsome exception.

Embarrassing, though. The stunned moment when Mary caught my eye as I inhaled her son's dirty clothing longingly will haunt me for many's the long day. The shame of all shames came upon me at that instant and I cannot think of it without squishing my head into my pillow and making little squeaky sounds of self-reproach. Which is exactly

141

what I am going to be doing from now until the
blessed sleep claims me.

> **REPROACH:** Accusation, recrimination. The
> phrase 'I can't believe you've done/are doing/would
> do/are just about to do (delete where applicable)
> this to me' is all about reproach. People who like
> to reproach would be lost without it.
>
> **SELF-REPROACH:** Giving out to yourself
> for various acts of stupidity and humiliation, like,
> 'How COULD you??' Or, more appropriately,
> 'How COULD I?'

MY FRIDAY FEELINGS

After school, I had my second-last session with
stupid Triona. She asked all kinds of questions about
why I skipped the last few weeks and how I felt
about 'the process'. Awkward, because no matter
how much you dislike someone, it is difficult to say
it to their face. But she weaseled it out of me, being
all, 'It's my job to be unbiased and neutral; this is a
safe space; nothing you say will have a negative
effect on me.'

She was annoyed, though; I could read it in her
eyes and in the casual, deliberate tone she used with
me for the whole rest of the session. No one likes

FRIDAY being compared to frogspawn, no matter how blasé and professional they are supposed to be. And once I started talking about how irritating and bland I found her, I kept trying to qualify it, which is where the whole frogspawn thing came in. It's something inoffensive and unhelpful and kind of gross to most people, but without it there wouldn't be frogs, so just because it doesn't help me live my life any better doesn't mean it isn't a good thing in a certain way. Comparisons of that nature don't really help, though, unless it be to help shove my size three foot in my overly capacious mouth.

Anyway, she was all breathing calmly and, 'It is interesting that you have developed these feelings of resentment towards me, Primrose. Why do you think that is?'

And I was all, 'I'd like to be able to say I was projecting some of my anger at my mother's death and my subsequent feelings of abandonment at you, but to be brutally honest, I think I just don't like you.' That felt a bit harsh, and she took her little notes down and asked me to elaborate.

'Your persona, the way you are, or the way you choose to operate in the context of the counselling process, it has made me feel increasingly alienated and frustrated throughout the whole of our time together and I would appreciate if you could

143

recommend an alternative therapist, perhaps one with whom I would be more compatible.'

Wow! I did not know I had it in me to be so coherent in her office. I would have high-fived myself in pride if I hadn't felt so awkward and also reluctant to act in irrational ways that would give her an excuse to explain away my feelings.

So there's this group thing, run by a colleague of hers, where as well as an hour a week of one-on-one talk with a counsellor-type person, there's a group session, with five or so other 'troubled' kids, where you do crafts and things and also talk about stuff, which she called 'peer-on-peer verbal exchanges'. (See why I had to be all articulate? It's the only language the robot lady understands.)

144

Anyway, she's going to call her and try to get me in within the month, which is decent of her. And next week I'm to come back for our final session, where she's going to tell me what's in the report she's sending on, and we can decide what the main points I have to work on over the coming year will be. So that went kind of well, really. I told Dad about it and he said that he wants me to feel comfortable, so anything that helps me in that line is all right by him. Which is the least annoying thing he could have said.

I probably picked a good week to get all stroppy with Triona, because of the trial and everything. I kind of just don't give a hoot any more. I just feel like I should be more open about who I am or what I want or something, because life is short and drivers are drunk and so on and so bleh. I wonder how Brian McNasty-pants is handling the prison lifestyle? I hope his family aren't too lonely after him. It must be strange to have a parent in jail, kind of like they died or left the family, but finite. Who knows? Maybe one day I could experience it myself if anyone goes through Daddy Dearest's books, although he probably keeps his business dealings and tax-thingies nice and legal, only fiddling what the government says he can and suchlike. Which is good, because if he was a criminal I would be well on my way to being an orphan, like Mary Lennox, or Sara Crewe, or Harry Potter, only without a walled garden to work in, or a secretly alive daddy, or magic powers and a terrible enemy. I would not like to be an orphan because there'd be no one to take me in. Well, maybe a few people, but not anyone I know that well, except maybe Anne. It would be cool, being Joel's kind-of sister. Hmmm ...

CAPACIOUS: Big, great big, great big stupid gaping, and so on. Not small. If a thing is capacious you can fit a lot of biscuits in it.

BABY LOVE

Sitting in the kitchen, watching Phineas sleep. The elders, in their wisdom, have decided I am old enough to babysit him while they repair to the pub down the road to drink and 'catch up'. He is a small and delightful man and smells all fragile and loveable. This is a cunning ruse. He likes to pull my hair and his vice-like grip is hard to get out of if, like me, you have some reservations about punching babies repeatedly in the face.

It's hard to know how I feel about Phineas. It's hard not to remember that he is as old as Mum is dead, being born on the day of the funeral and all. So I'm not really able to put that out of my head when I look at him, which isn't a good or bad thing, it's just a thing that I think about a bit and don't mention to his parents on account of not wanting them to think I'm all morbid and junk.

Éanna and Patsy are really nice. We had a big fry this morning and they let me help with the cooking (which was interesting) and not the washing-up (which is always boring and kind of samey – actually, I think washing-up is a big part of why the Daddy-Man does not cook often). Still not sure how the week and a half with them at Christmas time will go, though. It will be weird and isolated and Joel-less. Very glad we're back talking and hanging out and doing fun stuff. Which reminds me, I am totally going to put moustaches on Phineas and take photos, now that everyone is out of the way.

BABY ADOLF

Guess which moustache became adhered to the innocent baby face of my only small cousin? The WORST one; not the groucho, or the gentleman thief or even the Freddie Mercury (which oddly kind of suited his features). No, that would have been quasi-explainable and not a terrible insult to the baba-man who is now awake and crying and looking like the evilest dictator of a baby that ever there was, as I try to remove the small black square from his upper lip.

However this ends, I am guessing it will not be well. I have tried baby lotion, water, milk, the expensive exfoliating stuff Dad pretends he doesn't use and also the age-old art of tugging. Gently, of course – he is only small and I don't want to hurt him. Well, at this stage I wouldn't mind hurting him a little, but only to conceal the evidence of my terrible crime.

Why do embarrassing things involving things sticking to things always happen to me? They don't happen to other people. Maybe they do, though. I mean, I'm hardly likely to tell anyone about this once it's sorted, and I certainly won't be telling anyone about the duct tape incident. Because it never happened. I may tell Joel about this, though. Because putting moustaches on babies is kind of our thing, and he should know that it can sometimes culminate in tragedy. It *is* kind of funny, all the same. Might get the camera out one more time ...

GUESS WHO'S NOT GOING TO MAYO?

Go on! Guess. It is an awfully easy one. Patsy and Dad thought it was quite funny, actually. But Éanna works in the field of human rights, and the fact that it was that particular moustache really got to her. She was going on about how she didn't want her child to be karmically linked to a monster while he was still in the cradle. Which is fair enough, except for the 'karmically linked' bit, which reeks of hippie. Éanna and Mum's friend Sorrel would probably get on well, actually.

But anyway, she was a bit tipsy – they all were – and then she got kind of mad with Dad for not giving out to me enough. To be fair, he did try, but he was also busy trying to keep a straight face. Which annoyed Éanna a lot more than the moustache. Apparently she was up till six a.m. trying to get the moustache off him and couldn't do it. Then this morning he had pulled it off himself and was happily trying to eat it and cried when she took it away. Phineas might just be the best cousin ever.

GENETIC CODE: The sciencey bits that make stuff stuff. Like I have a different genetic code to Ciara and even Joel, even though we all share a love of wigs and many other delightful things. If Mum and Dad had had another child, it would have a genetic code that was like mine, but with different bits. Like, it might have gotten Dad's fashion sense, or Mum's inability to pick me up from school on time, instead of just getting the awesome bits like *moi*.

149

Dad will give out to me tomorrow, though, now that he has to sort a new place for me to stay while he and Hedda gad about NYC, taking yellow cabs and buying shoes and getting mugged and doing other things that people do in New York. I might get to go! Although, honestly, I doubt it. I have no place in Fintan's romantic break. Also, I would totally get up to something. It's just the way I am, I can't help it. I do kind of resent not being invited. I mean, I've known him way longer than Hedda has, and share parts of his genetic code, much and all as I'd sometimes rather not ...

HA

Fintan just asked me for a copy of one of the Hitler photos. He is using it as his screen-saver on the laptop. He says it is so he can look 'long and hard at it' next time I ask for a favour. It's a pathetic excuse for an excuse – the man can hardly glance at it without snorting unattractively. Lucky Hedda's not around to see that or he'd be going to NY all alone, like a loser. Although I do want to ask him for a favour, as it happens. The Deep Tinkers are playing at a coffee shop on Sunday morning, and Joel and me wanted to go for breakfast there (with a parent who'd sit good and far away, if necessary). Maybe if I convince him it's all about the music ... If he realises that I am all about the hot, hot Felix he will not be best pleased.

Or he will think it's adorable and josh me about it good-heartedly, with hair-ruffling and suchlike. Oh God, that would be hell! He'd totally tell people too. He'd be like, 'My little girl is growing up,' or he'd call Felix 'your young man', when he is not and he never will be, due to the fact that he is so much older and more sophisticated than small, childish me and the fact that I am not a vampire lady in a catsuit. Also, my semi-stalking him could put a bit of a dampener on any possible relationship. I mean, if he ever was to find out that I secretly smell his T-shirts when he is out of the room, I imagine he

would be more scared than flattered. Plus, Mary wouldn't be able to mind me any more if that kind of thing was allowed to escalate. It would be a conflict of interest. In a hot way. Sigh. I am such a loser; can't believe I'm obsessing this much. And about Ella's brother. Eek.

I planned a mix CD for him last night. It was going to be all vaguely dark and creepy pop songs and I was going to put purple stars and gold swirls on the cover, and gold stars and purple swirls on the CD itself. Then I realised that he would totally find out it was me. And then my stalking would be at an end and I would probably have to do my homework in Ella's room, where nothing smells of foxy. I will ring Joel and strategise. Maybe I can pretend that it is he who wants to hold Felix's hand and be taken on a tour of his iTunes library. Ooh-er. No, deceit could just lead to rowing and not speaking. And that would suck. I'm totally going to suggest that I stay with Joel for Christmas. That would be amazing, and me and him and Ciara could do stuff.

LATER

Went for breakfast. Saw band. The Deep Tinkers are kind of an Afro-Celtic fusion rock band. There was a LOT going on, but *none* of it was cool. My stalking frenzy kind of flew away once Felix was all red-faced and playing the tin whistle, with his ridiculous flicky hair. Also, Ciara turned to me and said 'I'd like to be that tin whistle,' and did a big wink. I'm sorry, WHAT?

In other news, Hedda liked them, Dad did not, and was pleased that I didn't, as it meant that he 'won'. They also sat at a different table to us and everything. He was almost decent and has not referred to the Phineas Affair all day. Well done, sir! Also, after breakfast, we got to go to a market, and Ciara and Joel came too and we all bought wigs. Mine is a purple bob, Ciara's is long and blonde and Joel's is a frosty mullet of doom, which is rather intimidating. I got a new T-shirt as well and some moisturiser that smells like vanilla and cinder toffee. Ciara and Joel both kept saying they wanted to lick me. I told them not to be so gay and un-gay respectively.

I am organising my books and CDs according to colour, darkest to lightest. My shelves will look pretty when I am finished. Roderick is on my bed, wearing a black waistcoat made of sock and eating a Deep Tinkers flyer. He does not look very impressed either. I suppose being in a band is still sort of cool. Afro-Celtic rhythms, though. Oh dear.

I wish I could play an instrument. I've tried out Dad's guitars a few times but I kind of don't know how to make them make sounds that blend together to make a song. I can make, like, two or three really nice resonanty strums and then it's all bleurrr gghhhh. Even when I did piano I always had to look at the sheet music really closely and practise so hard to get stuff right. It doesn't come naturally to me, I suppose, and I'd love if it did.

Perhaps I could just be the lead singer, who has nice black hair and sometimes wears a wig and smells like delicious moisturiser. I did actually taste it, once I got home, and it's kind of yeuchy, which

153

is good, because it would be an expensive habit to get into and would bring me nothing but trouble. Like Ciara with her hair. Although it's been a while since I've seen her chewing away at it. She told me her mother threatened to shave her head, which is not very nice, but she was probably at the end of her tether, what with everything having to be so perfect all the time; the only hair out of place was the hair in Ciara's mouth. Still not a very nice thing to say, though. Although Fintan has, on occasion, threatened to flay me 'and that blasted rat' alive, which would hurt more. I think that was after I fed Roderick one of his ties. I think I retorted by screaming, 'You wouldn't dare! I'll ring Childline! No wonder my mother hated you!' and other such words of wisdom. What a loveable scamp I am!

GOSSIP!

Today Ciara and I saw Lucrezia's boyfriend. It was a man in a car who picked her up anyway, and there was a hug! He did not look like Lucrezia's boyfriend should look (all darkly brooding and leather-jacketed, like a poet who also fights crime). He looked a bit tubby and a lot cute, like a librarian who bakes cakes at the weekend. We have decided that he fits the teachery bit of her, but not the rock-and-roll, tattooed hellion bit. I

would like to be a rock and roll tattooed
hellion when I grow up. But I would like a
crime-fighting cake-baking poet boyfriend
who doesn't really fight crime because I
would be sad if he got into an accident what
with us being so in love and all. Hypothetical
boys are the nicest ones.

Ciara got kissed! On the mouth, no tongues,
but they're thinking of trying that sometime
soon. She calls it French kissing, but I do not
like that phrase because it reminds me of snails
and frogs and other slimy things that French
people eat that are a bit like tongues. I call it
sliming. But only to annoy her. Her and
Syzmon hold hands and walk to the bus from
school together almost every day now. But
they spend break apart because she likes to
talk to me about him and analyse things he
says. Like, 'You are pretty,' and 'You have soft
hair.' Seriously. This is the kind of nonsense I
have to listen to. But it is good that her mother
did not shave her head. Although she would
still be adorable, she would totally have gone
on and on about it and driven me demented.
They are very cute, though. He sometimes
calls over to her house to watch cartoons and
play computer when their homework is done.
She is better than him on the Xbox, but he is

155

better than her on the Wii. I am happy for her, but long for a time when she was less cutesy and we would complain about stuff. Also, I would like a special boy for me. Although not Syzmon, who is a boy who likes to talk about football. Ciara knows quite a bit about football now. It is a bit disconcerting. They have only been kissing since Sunday and already she is changing for her man. Well, her boy. If she were kissing a man, I would be a lot more concerned and would have to tell her parents and possibly the police. Also, gross!!

Siobhán and Ciara had a big chat. Siobhán called over to her house and was all moaning about how her dad lost his job and how Karen wouldn't stop making catty comments about it, and when they go round the shops on the weekends how she's not able to afford to buy clothes and stuff any more. She used to get seventy-five euro a week pocket money. That is INSANE! She is worried that the other two will start ignoring her, like they did to Ciara earlier in the year. She pretty much flat out said exactly that to Ciara. Ugh, that would have made me so angry, like 'Will you be my back-up friend now that I am worried my cool (and by cool I mean petty) friends are ditching me?' Ciara told me Karen was always letting Siobhán pay for stuff, like hot chocolates in town. What a user. I told Ciara to mind herself, because getting stuck in the middle of ex-best friend drama is not what she needs right now.

Karen is moving back to hell where she belongs. Only messing – I wish. But she is being mean to Ciara and me. The Axis of Evil is going through a rough patch, probably because their tiny hearts can no longer bear the strain of all the fondness and this thing that humans call love. It is hard to be nice to someone else the whole time when you're basically a bully who takes pleasure in making people cry and eat their lunch in toilet cubicles just so they can avoid you.

157

On the plus side, they are busy having dramatic tiffs and no longer take the time out to pick on people. Well, except for Ciara and me for some reason. Someone told Karen about the whole Joel being my boyfriend thing and she keeps coming over and asking me about it in this kind of sly way, like she's waiting for me to say something she can pick up on to cause trouble. Luckily, Ciara is not a total ditz. I have made her promise never to tell Karen anything about the fight I had with Joel on pain of me burning her *High School*

Musical DVDs and letting Roderick loose in her hat drawer for twenty minutes (He can only hold his wee in for about ten).

So, as far as Karen is concerned, me and Joel were all about each other and now we're not any more, but we are friends. Guess what she said to me? 'It's nice that some boys realise that looks aren't everything.' Ahem. My looks are fine. I mean, I'm not all lip gloss and visible bra straps, but that is because I am not a tacky hell-witch that everybody hates, even her own friends. She will totally rule over a small and miserable country when she grows up. I hope it's far away.

Ella is hanging out with Ciara and me at lunch times more and more now. She used to go off to a special room with Maugie,but now she seems to be okay on her own unless she's been having a bad day. She doesn't say much, except for sometimes when she won't shut up about her cat. But I don't mind because Mr Cat is kind of amazing. He is a man, as it turns out, with proud man bits and pieces that Mary wants to pay someone to chop off as soon as he's old enough. She thinks it will mellow him out. But I have my doubts. He has a fine deep miaow and likes to curl up in high places and then jump down and surprise people.

Also, he will wait until you have got to the point of absolute comfiness on the couch and then scratch at you and ask to be let out, and when you get up he will steal your seat and look at you, like, 'In fairness, dude, what were you expecting?' He is like if Karen were a tomcat, only somehow adorable. And he has the shiniest fur. Ella is coming over to my house on Saturday for an hour so she can see Roderick. I will not let Roderick within a mile of Mr Cat. He would get eaten or recruited into a life of crime. But mostly eaten.

I have a lot lot lot of homework. Which isn't all that interesting but I have to go and do it. Especially the stupid French sentences, which are easy but involve a whole lot of writing down things that I know already, like where I live and what age I am and how many brothers and sisters I haven't. *Je suis enfant unique et je ne veux pas faire mes devoirs.* Instead, *je voudrais un pain au chocolat, s'il vous plaît. Hen?* ('*Hen?*' is French for 'huh?' apparently, although at times I suspect the teacher is screwing with us.)

159

MEOW-OVERS AND A BLOODY FANTASTIC TEDDY

Ella and I are playing a game. The game is called 'put the small jumper on Mr Cat and then take a photograph'. Mr Cat is not playing the game. Mr Cat is not a fan of the game at all. We were getting rid of some of Ella's old teddies to go to a charity shop, and I happened to notice that one of them, a black fellow in a plaid jumper, was about the same size as Mr Cat. 'You know, Ella, this fellow ... '

'You mean Mr Black.'

' ... is about the same size as Mr Cat.'

'And he doesn't need a jumper because he is not alive.'

'Are you thinking what I'm thinking?'

'How could I possibly know what you are thinking?'

But she totally was, or at least was open to the idea of making Mr Cat more presentable. We plotted our moves carefully, stripping the teddies that had the cat-friendliest items of clothing: Ms Ballet, Mr Black and Kermit the Dog, a teddy in an Ireland jumper that used to belong to Felix. Then we pounced on poor

HELLION: a lady hellraiser, someone who knows how to have a good time in a dangerous way. Intimidating, tough, but kind of fun. Cannot be tamed, unless it be by a sexy Viking who accidentally kidnaps her.

Mr Cat. Then he did some pouncing himself and took quite a swipe at my eye. But we beat him into submission. Submission took the form of the plaid jumper and Ms Ballet's tutu. He is on top of a bookshelf, being an angry transvestite. Ella is sitting under the bookshelf, legs crossed, drawing furiously.

I would like to be good at art, but I am not. My people all have circles for faces and my cats have triangles for ears. I can draw things that look like what they're supposed to be in a slapdash, cartoony kind of way, but Ella puts time and effort into it. She's so concentrated and exact. I'd love to be so interested in something or to have a talent. I don't have one at all, unless it is for irritating the old moustachioed one.

I've been slipping in that line of late too. Surely the Hitler baby incident couldn't have taught me a lesson or anything like that? Ugh, how boring and predictable that would be. I must plot a plot of plots, and scheme a scheme of schemes. Although first I will wait to be fed. I think we're getting Thai tonight. I gave him the number of the place I used to get food from with Mum, which is TOTALLY not being disloyal to her memory. She would want me to have delicious food in my tummy. And would hate to

161

think of the place going out of business because one of their greediest customers had passed away. I wonder if I'll ever learn to make Pad Thai perfectly, the way she wanted to. Probably not, because I would rather eat it. Nom nom nom!

Also, when he got home, Felix went through the charity bag and was all 'MUM, I can't BELIEVE that you were going to give Kermit away. How COULD you?' and I gave the snort to end all snorts, and when he realised that I had heard him he gave me a look and was all 'What, Primrose? He's a bloody fantastic teddy and he is not going anywhere, except back to my room where he BELONGS, Mum.'

I looked at the ground and got that sinking, wobbly feeling in my tummy. My type is apparently childish music nerds who stick to their guns. When I said as much to Joel on the phone he was all, 'And there's not a thing wrong with that.' Joel has got a bit happier recently and louder and more himself, like he was before he went to that stupid school. He is trying to get Anne to get him out of there to a school like mine. (I did not say, 'I told you so,' but I did write it down on my notepad a few times.) He gets on well with girls and also with boys who are not asses. Although they've shut up a bit recently, which is good.

Liam is weirding him out, though, because he gets all friendly one day and avoidy the next, and it messes with Joel's head. I said it sounded to me like he wanted to be friends with Joel but didn't want to, like, get hassle over it or pick up any of the spare nasty that was flying Joel's way earlier in the year. We tried to decide whether or not that is the behaviour of an assfaced loser. It kind of is. At least I think so. But Joel is a bit torn because he has no close friends there, and he's such a people person that he needs to have someone around him most of the time or he gets lonely. Which is so not me, but it is the way he is and it annoys me sometimes, but it also makes him great and always up for company and delightful diversions like moustache babies and the search for the perfect song to dance to while you're a little bit sad as well as the perfect dance to do when you're listening to the perfect song to dance to while you're a little bit sad.

> **DIVERSIONS:**
> Distractions, things that divert your attention away from other stuff by getting in the way or being shiny and appealing and lots of fun.

He is coming over this Friday for films and hair-dyeing post-Triona (last Triona session ev-hurrr!! Woo-woo and other sounds of celebration, fireworks and champagne corks popping all over the place even though I am not allowed to legally enjoy either!!). He is staying the night too, which hasn't happened in ages because Dad finds our intelligent and hilarious banter annoying and probably also doesn't want the other parents to find out how late he sleeps on the weekends when there is no golf.

I went online looked up the hotel where he and Hedda are staying. It is called Luxury's Lap and it looks obscenely expensive. Room price is 'available upon request' if you don't mind. He better be getting me a 'bloody fantastic' Christmas present. Like a golden iPod or a genetically engineered unicorn rat with a horn made of mother-of-pearl. Or a castle! I would totally love a castle. I'd set it up as a retreat for starving artists just before they made it big, and there'd be woods and an enormous library and a butler and everyone could do what they wanted during the day, but every night we'd get together and tell stories on a theme. Portraits of my loved ones would adorn the walls: Mum and Joel and Roderick. I'd put one of Dad up too I suppose. But somewhere a bit out of the way, like the bathroom or the back scullery. I don't know what a back scullery is, but my castle would totally have one.

THE BEST DANCE IN THE WORLD EVER!!!

Me and Ciara just invented a new dance; it is called 'head, shoulders, knees and boobs'. We were talking about bras and getting measured etc, and it just *came* to us, fully formed and perfect. We have been banned from practising it in the classroom, though, even during break times, because the establishment wants to suppress our creative urges, which they totally won't. We are far too provocative and sexy for the likes of them. I quite like being sexy, for all that the idea of sex any time soon, or just in general, creeps me out, because yuck and *waay* too young and also because I just haven't met the right Viking to get my womanly pulse racing and my heart all aflutter and ooh! It is catchy, though, and is fast becoming the rebel anthem of the school underground. The school underground is pretty much me and Ciara. No one else really understands the joy of head, shoulders, knees and boobs. Syzmon would join in out of loyalty, except that he lacks the necessary boobs.

165

ROCKING AROUND MY CHRISTMAS LIST

DAD: A mix CD of some of the pop songs that he sings along to on the radio while he is dropping me to school and a book about some old guy musician he likes, like Bob Dylan or Johnny Cash. Also, some cheap socks with cartoon reindeers on them. Maybe a money clip as a kind of double-edged thing? He'd probably use it, though, especially if it was expensive. Or I could give him one of those charity gifts, like a goat for a family in Africa or some figure-hugging dresses for underprivileged and wiggly Brazilian dancers. Or both. And I'd draw a goat in a dress and a Santy hat on his card, or, like, collage one, because I have never tried to draw a goat and can't imagine I'd be too good at it.

JOEL: Again a mix CD, this time with all songs from movies and musicals that we like. It will be all hand-clappingly happy. A disguise kit I saw in town, with different kinds of facial hair and spirit gum, which is what professional moustache gluers use. I wonder how one goes about becoming one of those? I could honestly say at an interview that I had been preparing for this job all my life. I have, like, 512 photos of various babies in various moustaches now. I should publish it as one of those ridiculously big books that get left on tables in waiting rooms for people to peruse. It would be a *tour de force* and a *coup de grâce* and many good things that have a *de* in the middle and sound impressive. Then, maybe a notebook or a cute T-shirt of some sort. He's all about checked patterns at the moment, so I could get him something a bit lumberjacky? Ugh. He's really hard to buy for, because he is so picky and also because I really want to give him something he'll actually like instead of a token, where it's the thought that counts.

He is eerily good at present-buying too, the scut. But this year I will not be bested.

RODERICK: A box of mansize tissues and some day-of-the-week jumpers (cut-up day-of-the-week socks) so he will always know what day it is. Well, once he learns to read, he will. He is a clever rat. Some day I would like to get him a rat wife, but his cage is pretty small and so theirs would have to be a childless union, and I'd hate to deny him the joy of choice. I wonder is there any way I could take him to a pet shop and get them to line up their more attractive lady rats so he could take his pick? 'Single white rat, likes eating tissues and going for long walks on the bookshelf, seeks lady rat with similar interests for cohabitation and food-sharing. Must enjoy nibbling.' That's how I imagine his personal ad would go. Mum's friend Sorrel took out a personal ad once, but only because she 'wanted to see what would happen'. What happened was she ended up having to change her phone number.

CIARA: I have been collecting things that are red and white for Ciara. So far I have a patterned scarf and little cherry coloured cap, a lollipop and a compact mirror. I only need something small to finish this present off, like shoelaces or penny sweets or some such trinket. Or gloves that are suitably pretty and fingerless, if I could get ones to go with the hat and scarf. Me and Ciara like fingerless gloves, as they mean you can text and pick up change and even scratch your nose if needs be. Also, if you wanted, you could write while wearing them, which means I could be wearing finger-less gloves right now and who would know the difference? No one. Because they are that useful. If I find a nice pair, I may just end up keeping them for myself at this rate. I am a reluctant bestower of pretty things.

ELLA: This was kind of easy, as her interests are pretty specific. Although she is the one person, apart from Joel, who would actually tell me to my face if my gift sucked. From the pet shop, I got her a long and boring book about cat care. Did you know cats can get acne, just like teenagers? I hope I do not get acne any time soon, as I am a picker and would get horrible scars all over my face and have to go live somewhere away from the easily disgusted, or in the best case scenario join a travelling freakshow and marry a tattoed man. For Mr Cat I got a collar from the euro shop with fake jewels on it (green and red – festive!). How he will preen and prance in his regal collar of destiny and glamour! Oh, I also got Ella a new set of drawing pencils in the brand she likes. They were pretty expensive compared to other drawing pencils but they are the kind she actually uses so I suppose they are worth it.

HEDDA: Some Santa Claus earrings for a joke, and a pair of really soft, cashmere gloves in the deepest purple you can imagine. She can wear them in New York to avoid touching Fintan directly. I don't know if she will be spending Christmas with us because Dad never tells me anything, grr!

MUM'S FRIENDS: Cards, especially for everyone who came to the trial. To say, 'Thank you and I miss you and I miss her and so do you and Happy Christmas and so on.' Nothing too jolly, but nothing too sad. Like something with an angel but not a Santa. Or with a Santa but no presents.

MUM: Flowers for her grave, something brightly coloured and happy. Would it be weird to put a little Christmas tree in a pot on her grave? She liked Christmas – I mean, who doesn't? But I think it would be nice. The Grinch, however, thinks it would not look right but, like I said to him, he is hardly the expert on what does and does not look right. He got all huffy and said we could maybe get a wreath with Christmas roses and holly and things. We are totally getting a tree. And I am going to make it so tinselly that it will blind and astonish all the visitors to the graveyard. So there!

SKETCHED

Ella is drawing Roderick and I am preventing him from escaping. She is being very quiet, although she sometimes tells him to 'keep still' when he starts his usual disgusting grooming regimen. Sometimes I am glad that Roderick doesn't have a wife as he has the disgusting habits of a man unused to female company, like Fintan, who picks his own, far bigger, toenails on the sofa when nobody is looking. He gathers the picked-off bits in a little pile on the arm rests and sometimes forgets to put them in the bin afterwards. This is the man who calls Roderick repugnant. Judge not lest ye be judged, as the Jesus said to the someone else.

I don't really like religion class; it doesn't interest me very much at all. Doing an exam on it is going to be kind of stupid and pointless. Joel and I totally cleaned up at our confirmation, though. He bought a TV/DVD combo for his room and still had money left to put in the credit union. I put it all in my bank account, which I rarely take money out of and secretly call 'my running-away fund'.

Thanks be to God. *Very* last session with Triona tomorrow! It's a wind-up one, because the other thing doesn't start till the new year, and it's kind of big of her to have me after comparing her to frog-spawn and all. But still, woo! I am full of glee, but I also have written her a Christmas card thanking her for everything and so on, because Mum was very big on thank-you cards. Even though Triona has made at least two grand off me over the past while, there is no excuse for being unmannerly, and who knows? I may get stuck beside her in a waiting room or bus or plane some day and have to make small talk that cannot be escaped from.

But she is getting the ugliest Santa card. The one where he looks a bit tipsy and arrogant and not like the kind of man you want breaking into your house under any circumstances at all, even if it is just to give you presents and eat some cake. He looks like the kind of Santa a girl can live without. But I am giving her a card because I am a lovely girl and full of Christmas spirit, although not half as full as wobbly, aggressive Santa. I just couldn't bring myself to give her the prettiest card in the box. Is that so wrong? Agh, have to stop over-thinking these things. Have written the card, the envelope is sealed. No going back now. No Siree Bob Geldof, as Dad would say before chuckling at his own wit as he likes to do. Sigh.

171

Ella's mum is coming back in an hour and we are going to watch some reality shows about animal trainers that I have recorded off the telly. These programmes never feature rats, which is a dreadful pity, but I suppose they are not big enough to look interesting on film. Also, people are not gone on the wild rats, the kind that break into houses and nibble stuff and poo. Roderick is completely different from those kinds of rats. Like I am different from people who mug people and steal their phones. That happened to Felix last summer, just after he got a new phone. Ella told me that. It is a bit scary, although not scary enough to stop me from wanting to be let go into town by myself sometimes, to wander around and look at things without being on a schedule. I would not like to get mugged, though, but I probably wouldn't seeing as my phone is really old and stuck together with bits of Sellotape because the cover is falling off.

ALL HEAD THINGS COME TO AN END

Last Triona ever was weird and I have tummy wobbles of nerves about the group thing which will start up after the holidays. She warned me about it; she was all 'Give yourself time to adjust, don't make any harsh judgements too soon,' and all kinds of other advice which I could have given myself, but it was well-meant and so I suppose it's kind of nice? I did a LOT of nodding and smiling. And just before I left, I pointed to the bowl of sweets and said, 'You know, Triona? A fly landed on this one time; you might want to clean it,' and she thanked me for telling her and said that she would clean it, happy in the knowledge that the unexplained tummy maggots that had struck down her client base was finally explained. Or maybe not. She did raise an eyebrow in a quizzical manner. Open to interpretation.

Joel came over and we watched some *Buffy the Vampire Slayer* reruns and then a tacky old film with swishy dancing on it that was on TV. Then we got dressed up and danced around the sitting-room. The shiny wooden floors and open spaces so beloved of the daddy-man are very good for swooshing and swirling around the place. Joel wore one of Dad's suit jackets and a cravat. (I can't believe the old man has got a cravat just lying around the place. He is so weird.) I wore a silvery flowy old slippy night dress that smells of old perfume and looks like someone turned stormy water into fabric. I think it belonged to one of Dad's former lady friends, but now it's mine, all mine, muhahahahahahahahahahaha!

I wore my spindliest sky-scraping heels as well, the ones I got for Méabh and Frank's wedding this time last year. Mum didn't want to get them for me, but I whined and whined and whined, and I'm glad I did because they are amazing and every girl needs at least one pair of shoes that you might not be able to walk in because they are for dancing. They are cherry-coloured and make my feet beautiful and sad at the same time. Sad because they are a little small and also because when I put them on, blisters are not far behind. But Joel and me need to dance more often, it was so fun and I can't wait till I'm old enough to go out and dance properly with attractive suitors who are not wearing my father's clothes. I bet it won't be the same, though. It'll be all chart music and dresses that are too tight and fiddly to whirl in properly.

Dad and Hedda were around but they kept out of our way, although Dad did come in for wine just as Joel was practising dipping me. He raised an eyebrow and was all, 'Don't hit your head on the coffee table there, love.' I did not, choosing instead to wallop it off the corner of a shelf as I was twirling. My bottom also got a thump, as I gracefully tangled my shoes in my gown while trying to do a flourishy tap thing and elegantly fell to the ground like a dying swan. Which landed on its bottom. While trying to dance and not being able to. Anyway, fun!!

We stayed up late after we went to bed, chatting and telling secrets. Fintan insists we sleep in different rooms, for fear Joel would come over all creepy and molest me in the night or something, but one or the other of us always sneaks in for a chat until we're just about to fall asleep. When I stay at Joel's, I sleep in

174

Marcus' room. Although he is more likely to crawl in beside me demanding cuddles and stories than the hapless Joel. Shame on him. The tiny pervert.

I would like a proper first kiss, with a real, proper boy. When I said that to Joel, he pretended to be all offended. He totally knew what I meant, though. I would like someone who likes me back and thinks I'm pretty and makes me laugh and burns me mix CDs and all that niceness. Also, hugs and kisses on tap would be kind of amazing. Just think, after a while I could stop making an effort and not bother plucking my enormous eyebrows or shaving my cactusy legs any more. I am sick of it already and have only been doing it for, like, three months. That would save a lot of time and effort, let me tell you. Wouldn't it be great if hairiness came into fashion, and all the men were mad for girls who were hirsute and fluffsome like glistening bears? Perhaps not, but I do like to dream about it sometimes, as in that alternative universe I would be smoking hot and a great catch. 'Check out the fuzz on her,' my admirers would say. 'It's as if she has tufty teenage goatees sprouting from her milky underarms. Phwoooooar.'

DISTURBING

I woke up in the middle of the night and went down for a drink of water. Through the glass doors, I could see that Dad and Hedda were in the sitting room, holding each other and swaying to the bland jazz he likes to think is all romance and class. She was all snuggled into him and his hand was on the small of her back. I didn't bother mocking him about it because they looked so comfortable and also because I was planning on asking him for money the next day and didn't want to annoy him by confronting him with his age and lack of cool. I should make a graph about it, actually. I could plot how cool he thinks he is (very) against how cool he actually is (not very) and show it to people when they say he's 'not too bad for an oul fella'. Which is what Joel said when I told him, on my way back to bed, of the disturbing scene I had been forced to witness. 'It's actually kind of sweet,' he said. 'I hope I'm still dancing and stuff when I'm that age.'

I informed him that it was not sweet at all and that the image would haunt me for many years to come. 'MY EYES! MY EYES!' I squealed, until he hit me with a pillow. Then I hit him back, and so on and so forth until Dad stomped up the stairs, all charm and flirtation drained from his face, and demanded, 'Are ye ever going to fall asleep, are ye? And will you please go back to your own room?' in the culchie voice he reverts back to when he forgets he is a big city man of business and terribly urbane and important. We put our best 'sorry Fintan' faces on, and I slunk back to bed, but as soon as he went downstairs I did whispery impressions of my angry

farmer dad across the landing to Joel, until we finally
drifted off to sleep.

'TWAS THE WEEK BEFORE CHRISTMAS ...

And squeak went the rat
As I sellotaped wrapping
On Ciara's new hat.
The tree was delightfully
Trimmed with much care
By the folk in the shop
Who charged more than was fair.

Dad keeps bringing that up, actually – how much
he paid for our stupid pre-decorated tree. He
normally doesn't bother with a tree, unless he's
entertaining at home, but he felt it was important for
me. 'Half the fun is decorating it, Fintan,' I keep
telling him, but then he brings up how much he paid
and how he wants the first Christmas in our new
house to go well and blah blah blah. Well, I bought
a small tree and loads of tinsel and fairy lights in the
two-euro shop and I am totally turning my room
(and if there's some left over, the kitchen) into a
glorious winter wonderland, like something out of
an eighties Christmas video. All my favourite
Christmas songs come from the eighties. It must
have been amazing back then, all snow and glitter

177

and crappy woolly jumpers in strange patterns that are difficult to decipher. What do they mean? I wonder, as I watch them replay and replay on the music channels. What is Cliff Richard trying to tell me? Maybe if I just listened properly, I would be party to the true meaning of Christmas and learn how to make my father both holly and jolly enough to ... I don't know ... string some tinsel about the place and make his only daughter happy on THEIR FIRST CHRISTMAS IN THEIR NEW HOME.

Our first full Christmas together in ages, actually. Normally he does a stealthy, Santa-style drop: give the present, get the present, give a hug and say goodbye with not so much as a cheery carol or a slice of pudding. I don't like Christmas pudding at all. I have to mask the gross taste of it with a small ocean of custard to make it just about bearable once a year 'because it's the day that's in it'. Mum loves it, though; she pretty much has the whole thing gone before the nice Roses, and the nice Roses are gone REALLY quickly at Christmas time, what with the visitors and, um, my enormous greed for hazelnut whirls. I *love* hazelnut whirls with a deep, lusty passion. Mum says they aren't a patch on almond charms, which were discontinued before I was old enough to enjoy them, but Dad is a caramel barrel man, although he does enjoy the golden toffee almost as much.

Ugh, been writing about Mum as if she were still alive, or somehow delightfully alive again, which she isn't. I'm kind of feeling it more now; I mean, dwelling on it way more. The loss. It's not fair – I wish there was some kind of exchange programme where she could come down from heaven (and if there is a heaven she's totally there, although maybe she goes down to hell for the odd house party – Mum could be a bit of a minx) just for the holidays, with an option on until I turn eighteen. Not too much to ask for, Santa – get off your wobbly bottom and make it happen! I'm all sad now, not simply having a wonderful Christmas time at all. Bah, humbug. Bah, humbug, everyone.

I might festively cheer myself up by searching the entire house to see if I can find my Christmas present. And if I do find it, I will cheer myself up even more by moving it to a different and better hiding place, so Dad thinks he's forgotten where he put it and feels all old and losery. Muhahahahaha hahahahaha humbug.

CARAT AND STICK

Oh my God. My father is even more of an evil genius than I give him credit for. At first, I thought it was a typically obtuse disregard for his only daughter, but you do not get to be as rich and poncey as he is without at least knowing a little tiny bit about the way people think. Also, I have seen him cry, so I know he is down with the stuff we humans like to call feelings. Well, he's down with the love bit anyhoo, the love that a man can have for a woman who should know better. I'm not talking about me by the by – I am stuck with him, but Hedda is not. At least not yet. But if the shiny, shiny diamond ring in a shiny leather box in his professionally shiny suitcase inscribed on the inside with 'To Hedda, from Fintan. Always' does its job, then she too will be shackled to him. Eek!

It's not that I don't like her, but I feel that I should have been asked before he decided on, you know, A COURSE OF ACTION THAT WOULD HAVE A SIGNIFICANT BLOODY IMPACT ON BOTH OUR LIVES. Grr. Arrgh. Other noises of anger and frustration. Yarrg, for example. I don't know how I feel about the idea of Hedda moving in here, much less being a stepmother-type affair. I mean, she's lovely in small doses but I don't really want to be tied to liking her and putting up with her and being civil to her for a long, long time, you know? Also, if she's my stepmonster she might start bossing me around and telling me to do stuff around the house and not to make fun of Fintan as much as I do. What if she wants me to show respect to him? I literally have no idea how that would work.

I need to mull this over, possibly adding the orange peel of rationality to temper the cinnamon of vengeance and the brown sugar of vengeance and a dash of the whiskey of vengeance and all the other things of vengeance that you put into mulled wine. Well, the stuff Mum used to put into mulled wine anyway. It smells yummy, all simmering on the range. I wonder if Dad knows how to make it? He probably does. For one who doesn't cook he's a dab hand at mixing drinks – he knows what 'on the rocks with a twist' means and everything. If someone asked me for that I'd probably twirl around and spill the drink on the ground, which is where the rocks would normally be. But no more positivity about He Who Must NOT Be Engaged. I have some important plotting to do. To the rat cave! (My room, but rat cave sounds better for plotting. Though room sounds better for being normal in.)

LATER

Plotted for a while, then began studying for tests (Maths, Irish and Science tomorrow). Finished homework. Plotted some more, then had a sandwich. I don't know if I should confront him re: the ring. He'd probably get all preachy and self-righteous and

'You shouldn't have been going through my stuff' about it. Which, in fairness, maybe I should not have. But he should take more care or lock his room or something and anyway, we're not talking about the very justified steps I have to take sometimes in order to keep abreast of my father's life choices. We are talking about *him*. *He* is the bad guy here. He could not be more of a bad guy if he grew a pencil moustache and started wearing a top hat and cape all the time. And possibly carrying a cane with a hidden sword in it, in case he needed to murder anyone at a moment's notice. He'd probably love one of those actually; pity I've already gotten his present. Although I might exchange it for a lump of coal, seeing as he insists on stubbornly worming his way onto my naughty list like the tool he doesn't have to be but always ends up being anyway. Grrr!!

Felix rang earlier, actually, and so did Ciara. Felix was just making sure I had a Christmas present for Ella, seeing as she has one for me. He seemed surprised that I had already bought one for her but, I mean, of course I was going to. I see her more than anyone, between school and being minded and everything. He was also wondering what he should get from Ella for Maugie. I told him she had a thing for velvet scarves and dangly earrings and probably liked Celticky woman music. I've never really chatted to her, but if you can't judge a book by its cover you can at least buy it a dust-jacket that matches its cover

... or something. Kind of lost track of where I was going with that. But anyway, then I got all paranoid that he thought I was disparaging Celticky music, which I was, but I didn't want to offend him and his fellow Deep Tinkers so I kind of stuttered and apologised and he said, 'That's okay, it's not for everyone,' and then we talked for a bit about the kind of music we both liked and it turns out there was some common ground there, so before I knew it I had had a whole conversation with Felix without saying anything moronic or giggling maniacally once. Once I hung up the phone I giggled like a maniac because I had to let it out some way.

More giggling was to follow. Ciara rang with some interesting news. I didn't tell her about the whole engagement ring fiasco because I want to decide what I'm doing first and also neither she nor Joel are the best secret-keepers the world has ever known. So I'm keeping schtum, silent as the grave, quiet as a mouse and so on. I wonder are mice really all that silent? Rats aren't. They're always up to something. Well, Roderick is, anyway.

If only he could talk! He'd know exactly what to do. But he'd probably try to blackmail as much food and tissues out of me as possible before he

183

advised me. Also, he could get me into a lot of trouble with a lot of people, having seen me complain about Ciara to Joel and Joel to Ciara and about Dad to almost everyone. So all in all, I'm glad Roderick cannot be given miraculous powers of speech.

Anyway, back to Ciara. She and Syzmon have had their first row, because he thinks they don't spend enough time together – which they totally do; they hang out every day, but just because she isn't all hand-holdy and so on in school he's all insecure and moany. My advice was to break up with him, because who needs that kind of thing? Well, Ciara does need that kind of thing, apparently; she's all, 'What should I do? Why is he acting this way?' etc, etc. Halfway through the conversation, I realised she was enjoying her boy drama and there was nothing I could say that would influence her. She didn't want advice; she just wanted a bit of a moan because herself and Syzmon had been all happy and relaxed and now there was a bit of tension! And drama! And she finally had something to talk about and obsess over. In a way, he gave her the best Christmas present ever.

I also spent the best part of half an hour convincing her NOT to get him all the High School Musicals on DVD for Christmas. She thinks 'everyone should own them', but really? Everyone shouldn't. Ciara should, because they somehow bring her much joy. But me, Syzmon and other people who are not seven? Perfectly fine without, thanks.

Then she got all quiet and, 'So you wouldn't like to get them as a gift then?' and I was all, 'Hell, no!' and then she got even quieter and said, 'How about Joel?'

I then had to do a small bit of backtracking as I assume she had gotten the exact same thing for everyone on her Christmas list. Oh dear. Also, I totally have to let Joel know she's getting him a Christmas present so it's not all awkward and 'Oh ... I seem to have left *your* present at home' and then when you get home you can't find anything so you end up wrapping up half a pack of Skittles and two pairs of clean socks in a fit of desperation and I'm getting flashbacks now, so I'm going to stop. Phew.

Also, Syzmon hasn't 'officially' asked her to be his girlfriend yet, which I didn't know was a thing. I assumed if you were hanging out and kissing with someone and not hanging out and kissing with other people then it was kind of a given. Apparently that's naive. 'For all I know, he could have a few girls dotted around the place, maybe even someone back in Slovakia,' she moaned. To this I simply answered, 'Ciara, it's Syzmon,' and she was like, 'Oh, yeah.' And then we giggled some. And then she was all, 'Maybe I should read the texts on his phone' and I told her that maybe she shouldn't unless she wanted to be a psycho. And then she got all quiet and said 'Mum reads the texts on Dad's phone all the time when he's not looking.' I told her that was different because they were married and so on and that if she

185

and Syzmon ever get married she can be as psycho as she wants, because it will be a lot harder to get rid of her.

But eep, what's up with that? I would be totally creeped out if someone was going through my texts on a regular basis. So I suppose it's a good thing that I am not married to Ciara's mum. Which I kind of knew already because she is not Felix and therefore not my type. Also, I couldn't be Ciara's Dad because I am not ready for that kind of responsibility. I don't think I'll ever be ready to take responsibility for someone who can be as annoying as Ciara sometimes is. I'd have left her in a box on the side of the road ages ago, wrapped in a blanket and sadly chewing on a strand of her own hair, which she almost never does at all any more, even on the days when she is not wearing a hat or a headscarf.

SLEIGH BELLS RING

'Are you listening?' was what all the teachers had to ask me about 167,868,768 times today. I REALLY wanted to respond, 'In the lane, snow is glistening,' but it would not have gone down well. As it is, I got my first detention (Daddy's little girl is growing up). Karen and Caleb were all snarky and 'sucks to be you', which it sometimes does but not because of that – I get given out to way less than they do. I don't know how they get the time to be so evil; they should be mostly in the process of being detained or doing lines. School is not very Christmas-spirity. I am getting nostalgic for last year when we had fairy lights on the ceiling and dancing Santas on the nature table. There is absolutely nothing natural about dancing Santas, but I like them and want to put them all over the place and then take Fintan and point to all the shiny and happy and red and green and lovely things and say, 'THIS. This kind of thing is exactly what I am talking about.' He'd probably ignore it all and get a detention room of his own with which to punish me.

Speaking of punishment, I am still mulling over what to do about the question he is going to pop to Hedda. It's going to cast a shadow over my Christmas holidays. Which, Anne says, it's okay if I spend with Joel and her – we asked over the weekend, so yay!! Also, she booked Fintan for a week over Easter, because it would be weird to take money for having me over (I'm there a lot), but if she didn't ask for a favour back he would feel like he was taking advantage of her, maybe. (He totally would not, but I told her he would. 'He's a proud man, my father,' I said. 'He likes to pay his way. Just look at his ties.')

Ella and Mary and me went to a market after school – it was fun; they sold all kinds of Christmassy stuff, like wooden figurines and mugs of milky chocolate goo – it was too thick and delicious to be real hot chocolate and we got biscuits to dip in it and so on. Then we picked Felix up from school. He was talking to two of his Tinkers and a girl who was flicking her auburn hair and biting her lip. She looked a little like the sexy vampire on his wall, only with brighter hair and not in a catsuit.

'Who's the girl?' I asked Mary, unable to contain my jealous curiosity.

'Oh, that's Marion,' she said.

Cool as a cucumber, I said, 'I like her coat.' (I did like her coat, as a matter of fact, but not as much as I wanted to scratch her eyes out so she couldn't use them any more to flirt with my beloved.) When he spotted the car, he said his goodbyes, and she PUNCHED HIM PLAYFULLY ON THE SHOULDER! That hussy. Has she no shame? Ella told me that Marion has been to their house a few times to watch films and eat junk food. She is frightened of Mr Cat because he tried to seduce her handbag and scratched her arm when she scutted him away. She is obviously interested in ruining everybody's love-lives. What a cow. I am bringing a tin of salmon for Mr Cat tomorrow – he would be a valuable ally against my new enemy and it is important to curry his favour. When Felix got in the car Mary did the 'woooo' noise that grown-ups and idiots do to tease people about members of the

TO CURRY SOMEONE'S FAVOUR: To add aromatic spices and pilau rice to your friend to increase their deliciousness, should you ever have to eat them in order to survive a life or death situation. It could happen. But really, to bribe or flatter someone, to look for their support and friendship – possibly with a delicious curry, but also in other ways that do not involve Indian food, like laughing at their jokes or presenting them with fish in a tin.

opposite sex. He blushed and said, 'Shut up, Mum.' He is shy AND slightly rude to his mother. Sigh.

WITH MY OWN TWO PIES

There's no way I can win at this whole life business is there? I wonder why I bother trying. I even thought about ringing Triona today – that's how sad I was. She gave me her card and said to call her any time. I didn't, though, because that would be like admitting she helped when she didn't, not really. Because nothing can. There's nothing wrong with me, apart from that I'm going through what happened and trying to live with an IDIOT. A hairy idiot who does not give a toss about anyone but himself. Ugh. Ugh. Ugh.

When I got home this evening, Dad and Hedda were making dinner. I had eaten at Ella's house, but I had two mince pies and cream. They had Irish coffees and watched a film with subtitles that was

189

'not suitable for children'. This from the man who was so proud of my zombie-film tolerance on Hallowe'en – he acts so different around her, all parenty. It is weird. *He* is weird. How can he marry her if he can't even be himself around her? I went back into his room with my two mince pies in a bowl and looked at the ring again. It was still there. I was not imagining it.

It's all big and sparkly. I tried it on, but it was too loose for me. Stupid fat-fingered Hedda. I don't want her to be around if it means he's going to be all bossy and annoying and telling me what to do. I don't want her around anyway, not permanently. She's lovely to me, but she could be putting it on, like he is with the 'fatherly' stuff when she's here. Ugh. Grown-up love is complicated. Which is why it must be thwarted. But how?

Also, Hedda said that the decorated tree was 'lovely' even though it's all matchy and horrible and utterly heartless. It's not colouredy at all and the star on the top of it is also a mirror. That says a LOT about Fintan. A LOT.

I felt kind of sick after my pie-eating session, and also a bit sad.

I've been thinking about Mum so much these past few days. I mean, I'm always thinking about her, but it's hurting a lot more; probably a mix between Christmas and Dad acting the fool. Mum was always really sharey with me about what was going on in her relationships, sometimes over-sharey even, though not in a gross way, but I would know if she was thinking about breaking up with someone weeks before it happened, or when Joseph, who we later referred to as Ho-seph, cheated on her with the girl from his office who was mean to Mum at the Christmas party. Which a lot of mums wouldn't tell their daughters, and sometimes, to be honest, I'd rather not have known, but I always knew for sure that if she was going to make any big relationship decisions I would at least hear about them, if not be consulted first. Which is no bad thing.

Anyway, I had a bit of a self-pity session and a bit of a cry into the pillow, cuddling Roderick to my chest and scratching him until he made little chuttery sounds of calm, telling him in mean and gaspy little whispers exactly what I thought of him of the hairy top lip and how much I wished that Mum was still here and all the things I remember about her and never want to forget. I saw a film once where a kid who'd lost his mother said he didn't remember what she looked like. I never, ever want to forget what she looked like, how she laughed, the good things and the bad things and the way we were each other's friends as well as child and parent. Roderick nibbled my pyjama buttons and didn't try to run away. He was still licking the wet and salty off my hands when Dad came in to say goodnight – he didn't turn on the light, just said, 'Go to sleep, Primrose ... Is that the rat?' (He never refers to Roderick by name.) 'What have I told you about having him on the bed? It's really unhygenic and disgusting.'

He picked him up and put him back in the cage and didn't even notice that I had been crying both my eyes out all over the bed. Wading through enormous puddles of tears, the heartless Pa then shut the door with a bang. I hate him. I sometimes really hate him. I can't believe I have to go to school in the morning. Oh God, I wish I could just fall asleep and not wake up until he was in New York and all this stupid nonsense was all over. Thing is, though, Mum would still be dead.

Have to try and sleep now, though. If Lucrezia gives me any grief tomorrow I will ... I don't know, probably sit there and do nothing, like a fool. Or cry. I don't know. I don't like myself at all, either; I feel like I never know what to do and I'm always trying too hard to be normal or at least appear normal when I'm not at all, and maybe no one is, not really. All this thinking hurts my head. And I forgot to remind Dad that we should do something nice for Mum on Christmas Day, if he can bear to be torn away from the lovely Hedda Hair for more than three minutes. I'll tell him in the morning, much as I'd like to storm in there with a loudspeaker and tell him now.

Oh God, I hope he doesn't ask her BEFORE New York. That would suck. I'd have to pretend to be all happy while she was around so as not to insult her and then once she left, SWITCH! I'd turn into a demon with big leathery wings and enormous talons and swipe at him and growl and fly away. Ha, he wouldn't be expecting *that*. How *dare* he give out about Roderick! Roderick has been nothing but nice to me since Mum's death, apart from the odd running away and hiding incident, which isn't mean but actually kind of fun and takes my mind off all the other nonsense. He is a better friend to me than Fintan. By far. Hear that, old man? By FAR. Why is life such a laundry-load of sad? It's not the way things are supposed to be, unless it IS, and then things are worse than even *I* think they are.

193

PRESENTS OF MIND

This morning, Dad asked me if I was okay.

'I thought I heard you crying last night.'

I asked him if it was any of his business and went on a bit of a rant about how he ignored me last night and how, when he did speak to me, it was only to be mean and horrible. He was really taken aback and was like 'But Hedda was over,' and then realised that this was not a good enough excuse and said, 'I didn't realise, but you won't get very far in life if you keep on being so sensitive.'

Cue more muttering from me, followed by, 'We'll discuss this later. Now hurry up or you'll be late for school.' I hurried up alright, hurried up like a snail.

School went from okay to terrible pretty quickly, but I was really tired and just wanted not to be there. I got given out to for daydreaming, but luckily avoided napping with my head on the table which would not have gone down too well with Nunzilla, the talking ferret who teaches CSPE, or the tattooed lady – she was busy giving out to the Axis of Evil, which has been acting up. They'll start invading Belgium if we're not careful. Caleb especially, because he gets all fisty when he's angry and it's very easy to make him angry – by doing your homework or having something he wants.

Karen was in dreadful form and, at break, she decided to call Ella 'a starey little retard'. So I punched her in the nose. Which was wrong, apparently. Ugh. She was way more out of order than me, I think. Anyway, Ms Smith used her scary voice on me and then I got sent to the principal's office. She also used her scary voice, but it wasn't quite as terrifying. My hand really hurt, but it seems that wasn't punishment enough. I didn't really hurt Karen, but Dad still had to come in for a not-so-little chat with Sr Fatima and Ms Smith. Happy Christmas!!

It was horrible, and I know you can't go around punching people but words can hurt just as much and what she said to Ella was wrong. So I don't know why she was acting all victimy and stuff. Also,

194

I'm not sure I want to go into school tomorrow because there is a fair chance that Caleb will kill me and eat my brains. Joel and Ciara both texted to say they think I was right. Ciara must have let Joel know about it. She finds it very hard not to tell everyone all the news all the time. I wish she wouldn't, though. On the plus side, I'm not kicked out of school or anything, so woo!! And me and Dad did have a talk, although I no longer had the moral high ground, because Dad has never punched a thirteen-year-old girl in the face. Bet he's been tempted, though. I can be quite sassy.

I feel bad; I've never been violent towards another person before, probably because I don't have a younger sibling. Also because it really hurt my hand and didn't even make her nose bleed or anything. She did cry a bit, though, but I think that was mainly for show. I am currently in my room 'thinking about what I did' (reading and listening to music). Dad wasn't too mad at me, though. He said I went to school edgy and angry, and that behaviour like Karen's would 'test the patience of a saint'. Which it *so* would, since saints were pretty big on not discriminating against other people. Except people who didn't agree with the church. Also, we ate sandwiches made from the leftover roast that Dad and Hedda had last night – so yummily comforting.

I didn't say anything about the ring, but I did ask, 'So, how are things going with Hedda?' and he said,

'Alright, I suppose – at least I think so,' all smugly.
I wish he'd tell me, though. It would make me feel
like I was an important part of his life, as opposed to
just this thing he has to feed and clothe because her
previous owner had passed away and if he didn't do
the right thing people would think badly of him.

PEOPLE WHO THINK I'M IN THE RIGHT FOR PUNCHING KAREN

 Joel – obviously, he has to support me; it's like
a best friend rule. Also, he is not a fan of
Karen's.

 Ciara – see above. Also, Karen was really
mean to her, so that kind of adds cherry atop
the cupcake of my violent over-reaction.

Everyone who knows Karen – 'It was only a
matter of time before she got what was
coming to her,' I have heard people say. And
if what was coming to her was an inexpert
punch that barely hurt at all, they were
absolutely right. How validated they must feel.

Maugie – she took me aside today and
whispered, 'That little rip deserved everything
she got, but you didn't hear that from me.'
She also sent me a few supportive winks

during the day which made me feel better, as Karen and her coven were insulting me and giving me dirty looks a LOT, and Caleb kept putting rolled up bits of toilet tissue in my hair. And in the corridor, he spat on me, which was, like, uber-disgusting, but now I am a little bit out of Ms Cleary's bad books and he is back in – order has been restored in the magic kingdom. Anyway, Maugie was nice to me today.

 Felix – he said so this evening, when Mary was kind of giving out to me about what happened, in a gentle, 'I know what she said was wrong but punching her did not make it right' way. What's that you say Mary? Two wrongs don't make a right? Well, paint my face and call me handsome! Anyway, Felix said he probably would have done the same thing in the situation, and has done once or twice before. I was all, 'Really?' And he slitted his eyes up in a mean and sexy contract-killer in a TV movie like way and said, 'I take care of business; let's leave it at that.' And also, 'No one messes with my little sis, eh Ella?' Me and him are a team of crack fighters crusading for justice in a world gone mad.

PEOPLE WHO THINK I'M IN THE WRONG FOR PUNCHING KAREN

 Karen – because I punched her. She hates me even more, and is constantly acting the bully and saying nasty stuff. Which is nothing new, but at least before it mostly wasn't directed at me.

 Caleb – he SPAT on me. Also, he is going out with Karen, so he has an interest in her not being punched, as it probably did not make her feel romantic and cuddlesome. Hence the spitting, I assume. Classy fellow, that Caleb; she should hang onto him.

Mary – but she is not a fan of Karen, so I think she will forgive me. She went on about there being 'a right way and a wrong way to stick up for Ella' but I think she was pleased at the sentiment behind the punch, which

> **VALIDATED:** In the right, the feeling you have when you are perfectly justified in turning to someone and saying 'I told you so.' Or 'I told you this would happen.' This is not the exact same feeling as smugness, but the two go really well together, like apple tart and ice cream.

198

was righteous and protective, if also angry and stupid.

 Ms Smith – like I said before, she used the scary voice. Scary voice is not something I like to hear directed at me. So next time I will be more subtle, by poisoning her corned beef sandwiches and making it look like an accident. Karen's love of corned beef is one of the things I use as evidence when I am explaining to people that she is an agent of Satan. No human being with a soul loves corned beef enough to eat it for lunch every day. Karen's ways are alien and villainous.

 Dad – maybe. He didn't get as angry as he normally does, which was nice, but he did explain how 'violence begets violence' and the best way to get back at someone is by ignoring them and also doing way better than they do at the game of life. I wonder if he is a successful businessman, enthusiastic moustache cultivator and wearer of expensive ties in order to get back at some evil child who tormented him back in the Bronze Age when he was at school? If so, what a loser! Have to admire his single-mindedness, though.

 Me – I don't like violence. And I hate that I have so little control over myself when I'm

199

angry. Ugh. Although at least I didn't run away like stupid Brian McAllister. I hope Christmas in prison is horrible, and they don't get to watch heart-warming films or eat even a small amount of delicious food. Also, I hope his family isn't even allowed to telephone, because it's not like Mum can telephone me or anything. He should just sit in his cell, eating cold Ready Brek three meals a day while 'It'll be Lonely This Christmas' gets pumped out over the speakers again and again and again.

CLEAR AND PRESENT DANGER

Eek, lots of homework again today. It's like the teachers think we have nothing better to do, which I kind of haven't, seeing as I'm banned from computer, television and so on until I have 'learned my lesson'. Well, until Dad thinks I have. Personally, I think the lesson was learned as soon as I lashed out with my fist, which was one of those stupid decisions you know is stupid even as you make it. Also, he got REALLY mad about me getting spat on, like phone-up-the-school, demand-to-speak-to-Caleb's-parents mad. Fatima tried to talk him out of a chat with Mr Caleb's dad and Mrs Caleb's mum (no longer affiliated with Mr Caleb's dad) because it would do no good and it would be like talking to a foul-mouthed wall but obviously she phrased it differently. He is meeting Karen's doting and deluded mum and dad tomorrow. Ciara tells me they think she is a beloved and innocent princess who can do no wrong and anyone who says otherwise is 'just jealous of our darling'. Oh dear. So, not the best of days, although I did get to go into town after school and finish my Christmas shopping. Now all I have to do is burn some CDs when I am allowed to use the computer again and all will be ridiculously well. From a Christmas present point of view anyway.

Joel is in a bad mood. We have been texting all night and he has told me some pretty disturbing stuff about how mean the boys at school are being again. They are all pumped up with puberty hormones and the stuff that makes them hairy and spotty and vocally hilarious. (Joel's voice broke last year, so at least he has that out of the way. It's not like it went *waaay* deep or anything – it kind of wobbled for a few weeks and then evened out again. I did have fun doing impressions of him, though, but only to his face, so I think that's okay.)

Anyway, that makes them into jerks also. Or something does. Maybe it's the school. I don't think it's natural for there to be no girls around; I mean, we're kind of important in the scheme of things and scraping away the ladies like an unpleasant side dish makes things *très* unnatural and creepy. Although, it's not like adding a half dozen Karen types to the mix would help either. Arrgh.

I wish there was something I could do to help. I've been on at him to talk to his mum again about switching schools. But now he doesn't want to admit defeat because he says *he's* the only one who everyone doesn't like. Which is totally stupid, because how could you not like Joel? I think it's a few loud morons being cruel and bullyish and everyone else ignoring it so it'll go away. But it isn't going away and it's making Joel miserable. I wish there was a foolproof way to stop this; I even offered to be his fake girlfriend for real this time, but he turned me down.

I kind of understand people being mean to Ella more than people being mean to Joel. I mean, Ella is very different and really hard to get to know and her ...I don't know what to call it – condition? – freaks out people who have only ever been around 'normality' before, and even though being mean to her is like kicking an incredibly intelligent puppy repeatedly in the face with your stupid Karen boot, I can kind of see why she sometimes makes people uncomfortable. She sometimes makes me uncomfortable and, if you're a nasty piece of poo and someone makes you uncomfortable, why not be mean?

Actually, that kind of works for Joel as well, only he would make people uncomfortable by being lovely and funny and clever and strong. Joel is freakishly strong, and even though he's not great at team stuff, he's able to lift heavy things like me up into the air and run really fast – well, way faster than me anyway.

Also, his biceps creep me out. He sometimes gets all 'Poke them, poke them,' and they're really solid and creepily unsuited to his skinny frame. And I'm a little jealous, as my arms are soft and bendy like the arms on a Betty Spaghetti doll. Only they don't have amazing bendy powers or anything. I kind of wish they did. I'd love to have a superpower, something special and secret that only I had. I wouldn't put bendy arms in my top ten, though. I'm all about flying, moving things with my mind and being able to communicate with animals or the dead. Also, being really strong and able to go invisible. Wow, now I know what I want for Christmas! 'Dear Santa, just one or two of the things on my list would do, don't want to be greedy. Just, you know, omnipotence and the power to be kind of scary to mine enemies. Thanks a million, Primrose Leary.'

As if! At this stage I know all about the conspiracy of Santa. I don't know if Fintan knows I know, but if he still thinks I'm in the dark, there will be a greater effort made to make sure I get something nice, because Fintan may well be an idiot who messes up at every available opportunity, but Santa? He's just a jolly old man doing his best to share the love in a world gone mad with greed and war and starvation and people being mean to Joel (and sometimes Ella) and other things that Santa would like to change but can't, because his superpowers only extend to chimneys, time-bending and being able to eat a hell of a lot of Christmas cake in one night. Also, toy-making, but that's probably mainly the elves. Santa would do a lot of delegating and administrative stuff, much like the other man with facial hair in my life.

Anyway, when adults are pretending to be Santa, they have to do their absolute best, even if they're rotten at being parents normally, because Santa would do his best, and no one wants anyone to think ill of Santa. Because he's all pure and imaginary and good, like the baby Jesus. And also Scrooge at the end of *A Christmas Carol*, only Santa was never mean and bad and cruel to Bob Cratchitt. Which is why continued belief in the man in red is an economically sound choice. If I get in any more trouble I might get shafted to the naughty list, though, and be given a lump of coal in a shiny little box. I wonder if I could get one small enough to put in the ring box, actually? That would put my message across in a pointed yet seasonal manner, I reckon.

This has possibilities. I must consult Roderick, or little ratty scratch-tum, as he is known as these days. He is being awfully cute recently, way more snuggly than he is wiggly. Sometimes I put my hot water bottle on top of his cage to prevent him getting too cold, but I get worried that he'll nibble a hole in it during the night and get soaked to the bone. So I can't leave it there when I'm not around to supervise, and then he just has the usual fleecy blanket. As rats go, he is pretty pampered. Rat Santa will be good to him this year as well.

I like to tell him about Rat Santa; Mum made him up the first Christmas we got Roderick, when I was worried he would be forgotten about. He lives in the North Hole (which he nibbled himself) and has lots of helper mice, like the ones in *The Tailor of Gloucester* that help him collect delicious and pretty presents for all the rats who have tried hard to be good during the year. (Because all rats are naturally a little bold, he rewards their good intentions and effort instead of actual behaviour.) He tried to keep a list, but he loves to nibble paper, so he kept eating it up and now he keeps it in his head, because rats have very good memories and Rat Santa has the best memory of all. Someday, if I have kids, I will tell them about Rat Santa too. My mum really was the bestest. She would have been an awesome granny.

THUMB OUTSIDE THE FIST

Dad has had a meeting at school with Fatima and also Karen's parents. He is currently teaching me to throw a punch properly, like I mean business. It involves moving your shoulder and keeping your thumb outside the fist so you don't get hurt. Also, 'planting your feet on the ground'. He is pleased with my progress, although he was very clear about his disapproval of my behaviour. He is teaching me this skill in the hopes that I will never have to use it.

We have taken a break because I winded him with a blow to the stomach, which is literally all his fault. Who insisted on teaching who to throw a punch instead of allowing who to listen to music and make friendship bracelets out of embroidery thread? I will tell you who. My dad. (The second 'who' is me.) I still feel a little bad, though, and have cut short the lesson to dance attendance on the fallen warrior, who is sipping small amounts of water and looking at me with a measure of fear in his eyes. Also a little pride. He has created a monster, but now the monster can throw a punch. Soon I shall be unstoppable! For the moment, though, I am still grounded. Also, I think that in real life there would be no goading to 'punch me as hard as you can' while standing, arms spread, face full of a foolish eagerness for me to bring the pain. I do not think real fights happen this way, not that I have ever been in a real, proper fight or anything, but it just doesn't seem likely.

I might share my new-found skills with Joel, though, in case things at school get any nastier and he has to learn how to defend himself. That's a horrible thought, actually. I'm really worried about him. It seemed like things were getting better, but now they're worse all over again and I don't know how much of the getting better part was put on and how much was true. It is so hard to know what I can do to help him, apart from be his friend and tell him he is great and in the right and stuff like that, because it's not like I go to his school or even know the people involved or anything. Except Liam. I do know Liam to see. He was very quiet at Hallowe'en, but sometimes I see him in town and he's all tracksuits and shapes, like an idiot. I'd love to give him a smack. But I won't because violence is wrong and I know that now. Which I have said to Dad on more than one occasion, followed by 'Please, can I use the computer?'

'Not yet,' he says. I haven't asked him yet today, though, because I am waiting until he forgets the pain in his belly. I'm really considerate that way.

GLOVE AND WARMTH

Today was Saturday and it was really nice. I was allowed outside the house, and met up with Joel and Ciara – Dad gave us a lift into town and we went to Café Crème for hot chocolate and chatting, and Syzmon was in town too and Ciara texted him and he popped in for a while as well. It was really nice, actually. I have lovely friends. I wanted to talk to Joel about the school situation, but it's kind of private and Ciara isn't as close to him as I am, so I kept quiet. But we caught him up on all the gossip from school, and who is with who and who is being annoying (not just Karen) and who isn't getting on with who and all that malarkey, which is kind of not all that important, but fun to discuss and joke about.

Syzmon and Ciara were holding hands at the table, and when he was going he kissed her on the cheek! Which is quite coupley and also bizarre, because we're growing up and life is moving at a fast pace and soon we will be proper fake-ID-carrying teenagers and licensed to get up to all sorts of debauchery – this is where it starts, and so on. They were quite cute, though. Me and Joel made 'ahhh' noises when he left and Ciara was all 'Stop' and 'Shh' and 'Do you really think we're a cute couple?' She loves all that nonsense, being teased about her boyfriend and all that. It makes her feel special, which she doesn't get at home all that much because her mum and dad are always working or going places together and when she was friends with the other three she was hardly ever the centre of attention because that is Karen's job. Her hair is longer now; it's softer and it suits her, poking spikily out from under her many hats. I don't think my hair would look nice short. I don't have the cute little face for it. Also, it is good to hide behind and to keep your ears warm in winter.

When I was going there was a bit of an awkward moment, as the waitress was all, 'Haven't seen you here in a while; how did your mum get on in France?' and I just mumbled, 'Fine, thanks,' and told the others she must have thought I was someone else. Ciara believed me, but Joel saw through me like I was a pair of glasses. I sometimes hate that he can read me so well. Luckily, I didn't have to explain because Ciara was there so he couldn't grill me about it, but I think I am in for a question-filled phone call later on. Bah. I'd really rather just drop it altogether. But I can hardly say to the waitress, 'Oh, she's, like, dead and stuff, for ages, really. I just didn't say it to you because I would rather she were alive.' I mean, how weird would that be?

Anyway, we went round the shops for a bit after that. Joel had to get some sheet music (he is learning the guitar) and Ciara wanted some hair serum and glittery slides so she could do this twisty thing with her hair that she'd seen in a magazine. I didn't buy anything except some colouredy card and stickers to make covers for my mix CDs with. I am very broke after my Christmas shopping.

Then we met up with Dad and went to the pet shop to buy some food and bedding for Roderick and also to look at the adorable animals. There were parrots and ground squirrels (like normal squirrels, only without the bushy tail, just a sad little furry one) and tiny little hedgehogs. One was eating and it was the cutest thing in the world, all chompy and smiley. I was glad Roderick was not there to see me dote over it, as he would have been very jealous. We decided we would name it Leopold if it was a boy and Mrs Tiggywinkle if it was a girl. Then we had to leave it behind, because Dad was all 'The taxi is departing,' while tapping his foot and looking at his watch in a pointed manner. He was not immune to Leopold's charms, though, as he said in the car on the way home that Leopold was a stupid name for a hedgehog and if it were up to him he would have called it Mr Prickles or Johnny Rotten. He is not very good at naming things.

I am glad my Mother picked my name, because who knows what I would have been saddled with if it had been left up to Mr Moustache? And for the record, yes, I do realise my name is Primrose, and that that is not unridiculous. But at least it's floral, and I'm also likely to always be the only girl in my class/year/place of work with that name, which is cool, because I like being different. Although, not in the *weird* different sense, like I wouldn't like to be the only bald girl in my class or the only girl who always smelled of ham or anything. But being me is kind of okay. Except for the sad bits and the times when I can't get my hair to behave or my sums to work out properly.

LAST WEEK OF SCHOOL

And it's a short week too – ends on Thursday! We're not really doing much work at all, just tests, which are kind of easy because we haven't really learned all that much yet. Also, Hedda is not coming for Christmas. She is spending it with her family, so that is good. We were invited to Mayo (on the proviso that I never be alone with Phineas again and that Fintan remain vigilant and daughter-adjacent at all times), but Fintan is already skipping work to go on his lovey-dovey break of romance and proposals so it's just myself and himself.

We are booked into a fancy-pants restaurant, because 'no way' is he cooking and 'no way' is he letting me try to cook. Bleh. I suppose it'll be nice but it just doesn't seem very Christmassy. I am invited to dinner at Méabh's house on Christmas Eve Eve, though; she is making food and stuff and she said she supposed Dad could come too, even though he's a terrible fellow who broke up with my mother in the hospital when I was but two days old and is therefore to be shunned. (I think it may have been mainly to get out of nappy-changing duty.) She wasn't being rude, but Dad was kind of hated by mum's loyal lady-friends for the idiotic way in which he chose to end things and also for various other reasons I haven't been told about yet because I'm only a wee childeen and wouldn't understand. (I totally understand. If Syzmon broke up with Ciara in an idiotic way I'd gladly badmouth him out of friendly loyalty and so on and so forth.)

So anyway, when she was all, 'Of course, Fintan can come too,' I understood that this

211

was just to make sure I was definitely allowed to be there, because it would be a party with wine and stuff and a tiny helpless infant like myself cannot be trusted without parental supervision – at least that's what Dad would say to try and get out of letting me go. But I really want to be there, because I haven't seen Mum's friends since the day in court, and I don't want to lose touch with that part of the life we had together.

Also, they're lovely – Hedda might soon be lost to the dark side if she and Dad get hitched and I need lovely grown-up ladies to ask about my lady-body, becoming a woman, blossoming into a beautiful female flower that has to shave its legs and bleed mysteriously once a month etc. Because whatever about bra-purchase, that part of my life must forever remain secret from the moustache father. Because ewwwww! And I know, not 'eww-www!', more, 'a natural and beautiful part of a young girl's progression into womanhood' and 'nothing to be embarrassed about'.

But I am a rational human being, and when one is bleeding out of secret lady places, it's not something to be particularly proud of. If Mum is anything to go by, it is something to make one slightly fonder of one's hot water bottle than normal and sometimes more prone to cry at the television.

But that is totally coming soon (Ciara already has hers), and when it does, I want to be prepared, and also to have a grown-up lady who will come to Boots

212

with me without it being more awkward than it already is. Or maybe I won't need anyone. I mean, I could just go by myself. How hard could it be? Dad would have to drop me into town, though, as there's not a pharmacy nearby that I could walk to. But still, I suppose I always presumed one needed a lady to do these things with because I had a lady who was my mum. Who still is my mum, but is no longer available for 'coming of age' rituals. At least I've already got a hot water bottle.

Anyway, enough about that. I am looking forward to Christmas Eve Eve, because it will be like having a slice of the type of Christmas I would be having with Mum if she were still alive. Which will be lovely, and I'm so glad Méabh thought of me, but it will probably be a bit sad-making and memory-bringing-back as well. But if I go in prepared for that, maybe I won't make a 'holy show of myself', as Mum used to say, by wailing and snotting all over the mince pies and whatever stupidly vegetarian festive dish Méabh has cooked up.

I do understand the whole vegetarian thing, I do. I love animals, sometimes to the point of making ridiculous outfits and delicious treats that hang from the roof of their cages by colouredy ribbons. But I like bacon too. And sausage sandwiches and roast beef and all the other delicious things animals get made into after they die a perfectly natural death from old age surrounded by their families and loved ones.

213

Maybe it's the way they pass on, you know, into the next life – marinading and spicing to them is what being put on a burning boat was to the Vikings, or being given a neat grave with an elegant marker is to us. Or something. Enough of this, or I will talk myself out of honey-roasted ham and turkey (not a big fan of turkeys and pigs anyway, they're not a patch on rats for sheer brilliance and nerve, although they do make up for that in terms of yumminess).

That evening should be nice, though. Awkward as anything for Dad, but nice in other ways. Maybe once they meet him, they'll see he's not the worst, although sometimes he kind of is. Only a bit, though. He better let me go. He said he would when he was on the phone to Méabh, but it'd be just like him to have a 'work emergency' on that night, just to be awkward. Grr.

CARD-SHARK

Dad gets sooooo many Christmas cards. We've got 153!!! The most we ever got was 97, and that was the year Mum was working at the playschool, so each of the kids gave her a card, which upped our total by around half. I don't understand why people are sending him cards. Does he have a secret army of friends he rarely meets or keeps secret from me so I won't be jealous? At this rate we could totally make it to two hundred before the day itself and build a massive fort out of them and hide in it or something.

School was okay today. Karen came up to me and Ciara, wanting to be friends. She said how we're all growing up and shouldn't we put the past behind us? Then she grilled Ciara about Syzmon and me about Joel and Felix and anyone else I know who is a teenager with boy attachments. I think she might be in the market for an upgrade. Poor Caleb. I was worried when Karen was all friendly and stuff that Ciara would fall for it and be her friend again, because the thing about Karen is, she's evil – everyone knows and accepts that she is evil – but she can also be really, really nice and interested and make you feel all special. This is rare, and normally occurs when she wants something, like information or a loan of something new and expensive. I can see right through her because I am a horrible and suspicious gnome who raises eyebrows suspiciously when people are kind, and who looks at glasses thinking 'That'll be empty in a minute, so it will, and then everyone will be sorry.'

Ciara is all sweet and kind and once said to me, in all seriousness, that every stranger is a friend unmet (it's a magnet on her fridge at home, her family love that kind of nonsense). So I was worried that Karen would steal her from me and they would be best best bestestest friends and would stop talking and giggle when I came into the room (Karen is the queen of the stop talking and giggle). Also, we talked with the coven all break so I didn't get a chance to chat to Ciara about it, beyond a silently mouthed 'This is SO weird' and 'I KNOW'.

After school I went to Ella's house, and as soon as Ciara had gotten rid of Syzmon she used up all her credit ringing me and being all, 'What was that?' The good news is this: she does not trust Karen as far as she could throw her, and Ciara is a little pixie girl who cannot throw very much at all. We have decided to keep on her good side, though, because she is scary when wronged. I hope she doesn't, like, think we're friends now. I mean, she can think we're friends just as long as she doesn't want to hang out every single break. I think it was a one-time boy consultation, though. If she starts having designs on Felix, I will not be best pleased.

Speaking of Felix, guess who is newly single? Marion broke up with him for Micko, one of his co-Tinkers, at lunch time at the shop in front of loads of people. He skipped all his after-school things and is listening to really thumpy music and glowering in his room. This is the best news ever. Although not for Felix, at least not for the moment. Mary is sorry for Felix and keeps leaving delicious things outside his door. He is not touching them, which is a pity because I really want a Toffypop and they are just sitting there not being eaten, but it would be wrong of me to take them because I haven't been offered.

You know something? I don't care any more; I'm going to do a stealthy biscuit swoop. Wish me luck!

EEP

Just as I was swooping, he opened the door. Embarrassment was imminent, but he just said, 'Take them; I don't need them any more,' and looked all sad. (This didn't make any sense, as why would he have 'needed' them when he and Marion were a thing? Did he, like, woo her with biscuits? And how do I get me some of that sweet, sweet action?) I asked what the music was, and he said he made a playlist of songs with 'broken' in the title and was playing them over and over and over. I went into his room and we listened to some music. I sat on the floor with my legs crossed and made tappy fake drumming gestures with my hands. He played a little air guitar, but his heart wasn't in it. I told him some of the horrible break-up stories my mum's friends told her, the ones I'm not supposed to know about. Marion was really mean to him, but it wasn't in the top ten worst break-ups, because he is neither engaged nor pregnant. He kind of snorted at this, as though it were but small consolation. I asked what was going to happen to the band. He said he didn't know if they could survive this. He does not like Micko any more, but there is nobody else in the year who is a grade eight on the piano. Then Mary knocked on the door and said that Dad was here to pick me up. He is salting my game a little. But I am making progress. Definite progress.

TOPPER THE MORNING TO YOU

The weird parallel universe where Karen and Ciara and me are all friendly did not last long. I asked Karen if I could borrow her pencil sharpener this morning and she called me a spaz. Upon which that song from *The Lion King* came on the radio in my head: 'That's the cir-cle, the circle of life.' I got told off for humming during Maths. But I couldn't help it, because apparently I'm a spaz. Ugh, I hate that word anyway. It's a little bit more than mean.

Ciara laughed her head off when I told her. Not at the me getting insulted bit, but about the two-facedness of Karen and how she can't keep up her nicey-nice act for even twenty-four straight hours. She and Caleb weren't talking today, and she was all friendly to Lauren, who's got a brother in Joel's year who is an enormous nosebleed of a boy, apparently. Ciara was all, 'I *need* to find out what happened there,' and went off and grilled Siobhán who told her not to tell anyone, but Karen and Caleb have been fighting a lot (but why? They're both such lovely people, surely not!). AND there's an older girl on Caleb's estate that he has, like, an enormous crush on. He keeps going on about how pretty she is with her browny-red hair and her lovely laugh even though she is not Karen and he's never even spoken to her. And – this is the best bit – it's Marion!! It totally has to be from the description and the school and the name. I mean, there could not be two of *that* girl.

I feel sorry for Caleb. Actually, I almost even feel sorry for Karen. Oh, wait; I just remembered: she's a tool who insults people for having blunt pencils and deserves everything she gets. Everything bad anyway. If she got a tiny and adorable puppy, she would not deserve it. Unless it bit her and pooed all over her room. I like that idea. She could call it Brownie. Although I think it is a good sign that, even given my new-found punching skills, it did not occur to me once to hit Karen right in her smug little face. Which just goes to show how angelic, saintly and all round pure of heart I really am. I must casually mention as much to Dad, seeing as he'll be buying my Christmas present and all. Smooth.

219

SCH-YULE HOLLY-DAYS!

Last day of school! I feel all full of holly and jolly and Christmas spirit and junk. It's amazing what repeatedly singing carols over and over all day long until your throat feels like it's just about to bleed will do for your morale. If Tiny Tim were to limp round the corner, I would give him all 203 of our Christmas cards so he could make a bed out of them. And a new set of crutches. I'd give him some turkey, but we've none in the house – he is welcome to join me and Dad for a 'Christmas dining experience'. Doesn't that sound strange, like there could maybe be, like, dancing Santas and impromptu carolling and maybe eleven waiters waiting. I live in hope and also in fear.

Ciara really liked her present and Ella liked hers too, I think. She gave me a picture of Roderick wearing a top hat and looking pleased with himself. It is in a frame and I am going to put it on my wall right near his cage so he can look at it and be reminded of how dashing he is. I like my friends and am lucky to have them, not just because they give me fine things, but because they understand what is important, like the fact that my rat looks damn fine in evening-wear.

I can hardly wait till Dad has jetted off so I can stay at Joel's and get up to all kinds of scrapes. I like the word scrapes; I got it from Enid Blyton. It means devilment, but the innocent, almost accidental kind you get into when all you want to do is have picnics and stuff but there are smugglers all over the show and you end up exposing them and being thanked by farmers' wives who give you big baskets full of food to show their appreciation. This has never yet happened to me and Joel. But some day it will. Mark my words.

Also, tonight is the night of the Mum's-friends-meeting-my-dreadful-villain–of-a-father dinner. A lot of them never have before, so I hope they don't chase him with flaming torches or assault him with pointy sticks. Because, although that would be kind of fun to watch, it would not be the right thing to do, and would definitely put an end to any possibility of me spending time with them again. Maybe even time without Dad, once he discovers they're not all wild, unfettered, drug-dealing hippies just because they don't work in offices and finalise business deals in golf clubs and fancy restaurants.

POSSIBLE OPENERS FOR DINNER CONVERSATION IN ORDER TO INCLUDE THE DADDY-MAN

221

 'You know, Sorrel, Dad's tie cost more than your dole for a WHOLE week. Isn't that interesting?' (But only if I want him to get many many looks of death.)

 'Dad, tell Méabh about the time you hunted snipe with the rich hoteliers and convinced them to turn that sad old ancient monument into a hotel that only rich people could go to.' (See above, but it is kind of an interesting story: they thought they saw a wolf in the woods and got all scared and 'Maybe we should head back.' It was a labrador, which was also the closest they came to snipe-spotting that day. Businessmen should not kill things in their spare time; instead, they should take up hobbies that are not ruthless at all, like candle-making or puppy-grooming. I suppose Indian head massage counts as a gentle pastime, but it's not really something he does, more something he gets done to him. I don't think I will ever fully approve of it, because creepy!)

'Méabh, why don't you tell Dad about how Tibet isn't free? He'd only love to hear your take on it.' (Méabh likes causes. She reads two newspapers every day and subscribes to causey magazines. I could literally ask her about any human-rightsy horror story type thing and she would know quite a bit about it. Dad is not a fan of people with 'causes', as they often ask him for money, and even if they don't, he feels like they want to. Also, he dislikes people who know more than him about the stuff he pretends to know about, like wars. But I reckon he could totally feign an interest for the sake of not being hated. He's good like that.)

Something about money or business stuff. Dad likes to talk about this and is good at explaining it in a way that does not make you feel talked-down to. Thanks to him I now know what an economy is. Apart from a 'bloody shambles'. (Oh, he thought that one was hilarious. Must remind him not to make jokes.)

 'Sorrel, remember when you got kicked out of the flat for not paying your rent and moved in with us for six weeks? Tell Dad about all the fun you had staying in my room when I had to share with Mum.' (Dad hates free-loaders almost as much as Sorrel hates rich people who only hang out with other rich people doing rich people stuff, like playing Monopoly for real and making poor people box each other for cash. Not that Dad's that bad these days. I think I'm a good influence on him.)

223

 'So, Dad was telling me about all the reasons we shouldn't give money to people who beg on the street, even when it's raining and they have kids with them. Apparently it's all one big scam. What do you think, Méabh / Sorrel / Dave / whoever else is there?' (See above.)

 'So, Dad was teaching me to throw a punch, so that the next time I hit Karen, this girl at school, I can make it count. Have any of you

ever punched anyone because they disre-
spected you or one of your friends?' (Sadly,
this is the best idea so far. And also, I'd kind
of like to know the answer to that question; it
could be interesting. Not too sure about it,
though, because I don't want them to think
I've turned violent and spoiled since Mum
went away. I'd hate that.)

'Dad, you know when you go to New York
with your new girlfriend and how I'm not
allowed to come because I will only get in the
way of your fun? Will you send me a postcard
if you're not too busy?' (This is to be used if I
get really angry with Dad and want everyone
to hate him as a father, rather than as a
symbol of all people with more money than
sense. He would probably ground me if I say
this, Christmas or no Christmas, so I have to
use it wisely and only when provoked.)

'So, what do you think Brian McAll-is-terrible-
driver-and-mother-killer is getting up to right
now? Do you think they get family visits on
Christmas?' (This could be good because
nobody likes Brian McAllister, and also
because it is a play on words. It could put a
dampener on the night, though, seeing as how
he's a murdering drunkard and all. As you

can see, I am just full of Christmas spirit. They should cover me in tinsel and send me around the place to cheer up sick children. Ho ho ho.)

 'Dad, tell us about how regular Indian head massages have helped your migraines and saved your life.' (This will enthral Sorrel, but annoy Méabh and Dave. Not sure how Méabh's hubby Frank will react. He's relatively new.)

ALL ABOUT CHRISTMAS EVE EVE (AND SOME ABOUT CHRISTMAS EVE)

225

Okay. I may have done something. It was either something very clever or something very stupid. Either way, it was done out of love, as they say. Do they say that? Who are they? Why do we listen to them? Anyway, I rang Felix. See, I had been talking to Joel and he was going on about how he hates his school and how he has no friends and how he sometimes hates himself and feels all ugly and useless and out of place. Which will not do! I mean, I feel that way sometimes, but my natural setting is a little whiny and uncomfortable, no matter where I am. But Joel is, like, MADE of sunshine and play. He is like a stylish puppy dog who has been turned into a clever human by a fairy who owed me a best friend.

So I got all angry thinking about this and how people being mean to you can crush the bit of you that makes you think that you're kind of okay and would want to be friends with yourself if you were not you, but a different person entirely. Joel is the person who makes ME happy when I am sad, and I selfishly do not want it to be the other way around, because I am still sad a lot of the time and it sucks and no one should feel this way if they don't kind of have to. No one as brilliant as my Joel anyway.

After giving him a pep talk which involved listing all the things that made him cool and better than everybody ever, I was in a fit of righteous anger. And I thought, if only the boys in his year weren't so moronic. And then I remembered Felix, and I figured that he kind of might be a good person to call, because he has LOADS of friends and is at Joel's school. I didn't really know what I wanted him to do, because it would be weird to ask him to be Joel's friend when he's not even my friend (though we will one day be man and wife). I kind of rambled on vaguely about the trouble Joel was having (I didn't want to betray his confidence) and asked Felix if he wouldn't mind looking out for him a bit when they were back at school. It was a horrible, awkward conversation that kind of lost momentum after he had said he would keep an eye on Joel, as long as he didn't have to punch anyone or anything. (I told him he could leave the casual violence to me.

Because I am a tough and foxy lady. Notice me! Notice me! Notice me!). I think – no, actually, I'm pretty sure – that before he finally said his goodbyes and hung up, I had brought up radiators at least three times. I do not even like radiators. I was looking at one, the one that is in my room. That is my only excuse.

Anyway, I don't know how I feel about what I did there. But Joel must never find out. Because he would be so, so mad at me. He does not like meddling. I don't either, but sometimes I get the urge and it cannot be stopped. It's like a disease. I am already practising the excuses I will make when this goes belly-up on me.

Dinner last night was lovely. We visited Mum's grave beforehand to tell her we were going. Well, in our heads. Sometimes I talk to her grave a little bit, but not when there are people around, for obvious not-wanting-to-look-like-a-crazy-person sort of reasons. Also, Dad brought wine for Méabh, and fancy sparkly fruit juice for people who do not drink alcohol but enjoy sipping things from wine glasses nonetheless: me, and Frank too – not because he doesn't like it but because he 'used to like it too much'. Well, at least that's what he said when I asked him. I thought that was very honest of him. I like it when people treat me like I'm old enough to understand things – for example, if someone was thinking about asking someone else to be my stepmother I would be most pleased if someone would tell me that, as it would show that they were honest and not as bad as I sometimes think they are. Just saying.

The food was nice (vegetarian nut loaf, and loads of little roasted spuds and veg) and the kitchen was warm and cosy. They have this fat little black stove that looks like something out of a book of fairy tales and gives out a lot of heat. It has a basket of wood beside it and Dad was very interested in how it worked. Frank showed him, and the two of them pottered about, talking about predictable middle-aged man stuff like energy efficient things and football. Sorrel came by herself because 'men are pigs, except you, Frank, and you too, Dave'. Then she looked at Dad and there was a huge pause until Méabh asked if anyone wanted more black pepper.

After dinner, we all held hands and said a prayer for Mum, and then we went round the table and told one story each about her. Dad told a story about just after he met her when she was young and in college and used to protest things like injustice by not buying certain brands of food and also by occasionally waving signs about. But one time she got caught up in a big group of people who were very angry indeed and the guards came and one of them stood on her long skirt and when she pulled it out from under his foot, the guard tripped over and she got arrested and had to get Dad to come and pick her up from the station because she did not want her parents to know she was being all radical and activisty instead of 'keeping the head down' and passing her exams.

Méabh and Sorrel told stories about when Mum was pregnant with me and used to always be eating ham and pickle sandwiches and how, one time, they came home and she was crying at the kitchen table because there was no ham in the fridge and she really wanted a sandwich. She was always trying to knit me things as well, but they always got a bit lopsided and Méabh had to redo bits of the black and red stripy jumper I am wearing in a lot of my baby photographs.

Frank remembered the lovely speech Mum gave on their wedding day (she was the chief bridesmaid) and Dave remembered the nice way in which she broke up with him and the way she made a special effort to stay friendly with him even though they weren't going to be all hand-holdy any more. (I was proud of this, as she had practised the break-up speech in front of me and I had given her some advice about it. Like, don't tell him to grow up and get a job, tell him 'you're in very different places right now' like they do on TV.) I got a bit teary, but in a nice, loving way, and said to them that this is exactly how Mum would want to be remembered and stuff.

Me and Dad didn't go home till late, like two in the morning late. In the taxi home we chatted about

229

how nice the night had been because we had both been worried it would be awkward. (It was, kind of, but only at the beginning.) Before I went to bed, he gave me a big goodnight hug. Sometimes it is hard to remember to plot against him. I hope he tells me about Hedda before he heads off. I really don't want to have to take strong and decisive

> SCUPPER:
> To ruin or
> prevent.

action to scupper his romantic little plans. I will if I have to, though, because I need to send a clear message to him that I am an important part of his life and will not be toyed with.

GOLD TURKEY

230

It is Christmas Day and Dad is gone to the bathroom. We are in the lobby of the hotel where Christmas dinner will be. I am drinking a children's cocktail; it is pink and comes in a fancy glass and has an umbrella. Dad's pint smells of old man and has no umbrella at all. He doesn't seem to mind, though. The platters I can see the waiters carrying are gold-coloured and there is holly and a band playing Christmas songs. All the band members are dressed like Santa Claus. I am in tacky, fairy-lighted Christmas heaven.

We went to midnight mass last night, because it is tradition. We lit candles for Mum and visited her with a poinsettia this morning before we even opened our presents. It looks nice on her grave, which is the cheeriest and most Christmassy grave in the row. Not that it is not still horrible that she is even in there, but at least she is being cared for better than anyone else in the graveyard.

It was cold and empty there. We stayed there for a long time, being quiet. I took off my gloves and laid my hand out flat against the stone. It was freezing. Nothing there was warm or pressing back. At her grave is where I most remember that she is gone completely. I don't think there are any happy graveyards, and there probably shouldn't be any. I mean, if you go, you want people to miss you. It is what I would want. I would want people to be good and sad that I was gone – none of this be happy, carry on without me nonsense. I had a bit of a cry there – not a big, red, retching sobathon like I have in bed sometimes when everything is quiet and dark; a kind of white-faced cry, tears falling down one after another. A soft weep, I suppose you'd call it. Dad and me held hands on the way back to the car. On the drive home we didn't speak at all, just listened to carol after carol on the radio.

I got some nice presents after that, but I kind of didn't really care. Not in an ungrateful way; it's just they weren't as important as what's missing.

Dad's coming back now and I have to go eat golden turkey and diamond ham while feeling very sorry for myself. I wonder if the Santas know 'Blue Christmas'.

GOODBYE, MR MOUSTACHE

Dad left for New York this morning. Himself and Hedda dropped me and Roderick off at Joel's before heading to the airport. He was looking very smug indeed with his waxed moustache and his matching leather luggage. Not for long, though.

Yesterday was a lot nicer than Christmas Day. We ate loads of chocolate and I taught him how to play the computer game I got off Joel for Christmas. He let me take Roderick's cage into the sitting-room as well, which he NEVER lets me do. It was such a nice day that I almost did not go through with Operation Destroy His Future Happiness with Hedda. She called over, though, and they had tea and talked about grown-up stuff. It was okay. I was half-listening and half-destroying my enemies through a combination of strategy and martial arts, tapping away at the controller.

Then Mr Moustache dropped the final straw, the one that would have broken my back, were I a camel. Instead it strengthened my resolve to stomp upstairs and carry out my POA (plan of action, but I think POA sounds more like I mean business, which I totally do). What he said was this: 'Why don't you go off and play or something, Primrose?'

Um ... because I *was* playing? And getting, might I add, much higher scores than he had been able to do, pathetic excuse for a warrior that he is. I said, 'I'll go off and play all right ... play havoc with your holiday plans.' (Except I said the last bit in my head because I didn't want to spoil the surprise.)

I was silent and deadly, like a cat who is also a secret agent in a movie made for very small children indeed. They noticed nothing, not that Hedda would have. I mean, I presume the whole proposal thing is supposed to be an incredibly romantic surprise. If I was him, I would have just given her socks – you can't go wrong with socks, cos 'most everybody runs out of them eventually. She gave me an okay present actually, a really cosy pair of red pyjamas with black polka dots on them. They are made from something that is called brushed cotton but I like to call 'soft pyjama material of wonder and glory'. It won't, like, rock my world forever, like the picture of Roderick, or make me laugh till I almost puke up a lung, like the tape Ciara made of me and her singing 'Head, shoulders, knees and boobs', accompanied on a small glockenspiel she's had since she was a senior infant, but they *are* lovely. But not so lovely that I had to abort the plan and welcome her into the family with open and loving arms.

Dad gave me a big hug and slipped me some cash before they drove off and left me at Joel's. He said, 'I think I'm going to miss my little nuisance.' (He calls me that sometimes, but I don't encourage it because I have nicknames enough already, thank you. Also, it makes me sound annoying and troublesome, which is so not the case. Any man would be proud to have a daughter like me. Proud!) Anyway, even if I don't want him to have a very nice time, I do hope his plane doesn't crash. Which is quite nice of me, considering all he's put me through.

Joel is trying to find a horror film that will scare the pants off me, and also *A Muppet Christmas Carol*, which we will watch before we go to sleep so that I don't get scared in the middle of the night and start sleepwalking and disturb him, which I have ALMOST never done, but it was a good way to convince him to watch it. (Embarassingly it's one of my favourite films. I mean, it has talking rats in it and everything.) Roderick is cosy in the dining-room. He is not allowed in the bedrooms, because Anne has her limits. Pretty stupid limits if you ask me, but he's nice and cosy so I don't really mind.

Also, I have something marvellous and shiny nestled in my pocket. Poor Dad. I really hope he doesn't find the fake moustache in the little box until he is actually in the process of proposing. I had to

HAVOC: 1. Chaos; dreadful, mixed-up, confused and panicked things. 2. What people like me wreak on people who (try to) thwart them.

WREAK: Cause, make happen. But not in a good way. Like, you can't wreak a surprise birthday party on someone. Well, not unless you've poisoned the cake, or something.

THWART: Prevent someone from doing something, or something from going ahead. For someone to be properly thwarted you have to be successful at preventing whatever it is you want to prevent. In my case, I wish to prevent, or thwart, my father's proposal to Hedda. Or at least the ring-giving bit of it. The ring-giving bit is totally thwarted anyway. Oh, also, if you have thwarted someone's plans you may feel an urge to laugh like this:

'MUHAHAHAHAHAHAHAHAHAHA'. Do not be alarmed, this is perfectly normal and means you have been doing everything right.

leave a calling card, so he'd know it was me who did it, and that I disapprove strongly of his selfishness and carry-on. He will not be best pleased. I may not have long to live, or at the very least not long to use the computer and leave the house and so on.

So I intend to live life to the fullest while I still can. The first step will be making an honest man of Joel, or at least proposing to him in a Fintany voice, while twirling my false moustache and raising an eyebrow in a gentlemanly way. Then he can propose to me right back and I'll sigh and, munching lovingly on a handful of popcorn, flutter my eyelashes and exclaim, 'Oh, *Joely*, you've made me the happiest, luckiest, most proposed-to thirteen-year-old girl with a moustache in the whole wide world.' Which, I imagine, is almost *definitely* probably true.

236

TOP 10 REASONS EVERYTHING WILL TURN OUT FOR THE BEST, EVEN THOUGH MY FATHER WANTS TO MURDER ME

1 He is very far away, and when he comes back he will have jetlag and be too tired for strenuous physical activities like stabbing.

2 Joel, Ciara, Ella and Mum's friends would totally have my back. If I needed to run away from home, that's, like, AT LEAST six houses I could stay in. Not that I'll need to because:

3 Our house is ridiculously big. There are many rooms in which we can avoid each other. Also, because of my snooping, I am totally down with all the nooks and crannies in which a medium-sized girl could make herself scarce if the need arose.

4 Dead Mother Card! This trumps the Ruined Proposal Card by, like, a lot. A big lot. Were it a game of cards, I would be winning. Sadly the game of life is a complicated and unpredictable business which sometimes involves yelling at innocent, helpless, half-orphan children who were only trying to do their best to hold on to the one parent they have left in this crazy, mixed-up world. Oh, that's good. If I throw in a few unshed tears welling in my big, shiny, hazel eyes, I could have something there. And some trembling lips that are trying to be brave and not to tremble ... but it's just ... so ... hard ...

237

5 Hedda would not like it if he killed me. She just doesn't seem like the type who goes for criminals, petty or otherwise. And a dead daughter would probably, you know, put a dampener on any nuptials that may or may not (may not! pleeeease, may not!) take place. And they BOTH know full well that if there is an afterlife I will find a way to come back and

haunt them (and their children and their children's children... Oh, God, what if they have children? NO good will come of that. Ughhh) half out of spite at being murdered, half out of the malicious trickstery pleasure it would bring me.

Dad's text is kind of open to interpretation (no matter what stupid Joel thinks):

```
Primrose I am mad at u. Will kill
u when I get back. U r in a world
of trouble, u have no idea. C U in
4 days time, dad
```

COULD mean

```
Primrose,  u  have  stopped  me
making a big mistake. Thanks for
your foresight and wisdom. I will
give you a killer present when I
get back. C U in 4 days time, dad.
```

It is an accepted and sad truth of the modern age that the elderly find it difficult to cope with new technology. Who knows what the old fellow meant to say? Could be anything; very vague and mysterious. I may never fully understand what he means in it. (I am looking forward to the possible killer present even though Joel thinks I am in denial. He is the one who is in denial. I might have to break

our pretend engagement off if he keeps up
with this kind of carry-on.)

7   It is difficult to be a successful businessman in
prison. Unless you want to build a criminal
empire. My father has no desire to build a
criminal empire. The man wears novelty ties,
for God's sake.

8   I got him a card saying 'I'm sorry'.

9   ... AND a voucher for an Indian head
massage, which cost almost all my Christmas
money. But it will be worth it, because it will
soothe his temper and remind him of all the
calm, non-violent, twinkly eastern inner
peacey stuff he has neglected in his quest for
revenge. I wonder if I can get the masseur to
meet him at the airport?

239

10 I'm pretty sure I can take him in a fight, if it
comes to it. I have before – when he taught
me to throw a punch and ended up in a
WORLD of PAIN, as the pro wrestlers say.

PS: SOME MORE REASONS...

11 I can keep thinking of more reasons; there are
loads of them. I'll stay up all night if I have to,

compiling a list. And an escape plan. And a last will and testament. The one Joel has is almost out of date. I've gotten more stuff since then.

12 I am a master of disguise, with many many many realistic and wearable types of facial hair at her disposal.

13 He really liked his Christmas present. NOTE TO SELF: remind him how much he liked his Christmas present while he is plotting your destruction. If nothing else, it will be a welcome change of subject.

14 Think of the small furry orphan who would be left behind. My whiskered darling has never done anything (apart from occasional inappropriate nibbling and pooing) to hurt anyone. He is the innocent, loveable, furry-bellied victim in this cruel twist of fate. If Dad will not show mercy for my sake, he could at least allow poor little Roderick to melt his icy heart, if only a small bit.

15 Um ... I'll ask nicely?

16 I'm pretty sure he loves me. I'm his only child, imaginary Hedda baby nonwithstanding. He's

put loads of time and energy into taking care of me and putting up with my nonsense. So it'd be a bit rich of him to throw all of that away for the fleeting pleasure of a terrible and bloody revenge.

Plus I kind of love him – not the same way I loved Mum, but in a different, stranger and probably more annoying way. Also, he sometimes tells me he loves me, which makes me uncomfortable and 'shut up, you weirdo'. But it is kind of nice to know that someone cares and is still going to be your family, even when you mess up and act like ... I don't know ... act like I've been acting. And I think it will get better, the way we get on, me and him.

241

And that, in sum, is why my father shouldn't kill me because I stole his expensive diamond engagement ring and replaced it with a moustache. Also, he'd never get away with it – Joel would know. I forwarded the text to his phone for him to use as evidence and *everything*.

WHAT HAPPENS NOW

I am sitting down beside the fire in Joel's house. Me and him and his mum are reading and watching a stupid TV show about things people used to like in the eighties. We are mocking her for being alive back then, and she is denying some of the stuff, and going on excitedly about some of the other stuff. It is warm here and I am safe in my slippers and the pyjamas Hedda gave me for Christmas, before I ruined Dad's plan to ask her to marry him.

Dad rang for a chat last night. The chat was about what a bad daughter I was, and how, if he respects my privacy, I have to respect his. Where's the fun in that? Also, he and Hedda are not engaged and he would appreciate me not telling her that they were going to be, maybe. Which is interesting ... wonder what happened there? I told him that I meddle out of love, and also that he should drive home slowly as the roads are covered in ice and there was a three-car pile-up on the news today. He drives a stupidly big, black, shiny, German car, and I remembered reading somewhere that black cars are more likely to get into accidents at night time because they are hard to see. He said that I should not meddle out of self-preservation. And that he'd crawl home slowly as a snail. A snail with foglights, leaving a shiny trail behind him in the frost.